HIS DEVIOUS ANGEL

Mimi Barbour

Sarna Publishing

His Devious Angel – Book 2

Angels with Attitudes Series

His Devious Angel

Contents

Praise for Angels with Attitudes:

My Cheeky Angel: (4.2 out of 5 stars = 147 reviews)

My Cheeky Angel was my first read, but certainly not last read by Mimi Barbour! This grabbed me from the very beginning and did so until the very end! I love how she brings humor, lightheartedness, real-life situations and paranormal all into one! The characters are believable as they tackle everyday life, love and friendship.

This is a sweet story with whom Annie, along with her guardian angel, Celi, get through the ups and downs of life. A must read!

Reviewed by ~ sweepingtheusa

His Devious Angel: (4.3 out of 5 stars = 56 reviews)

"This is the type of story ereaders were made for, the kind you cannot put down. I laughed and cried and cracked up laughing. The hero wasn't an Alpha nor a beta, he was just right, which was refreshing.

The heroine was the perfect blend of the girl down the street and the women up the road. And if you own a dog you'll love this story. If ever a book had a perfect ending this one had it. This author will go on my "Do not miss list."

Reviewed by ~ Olivia Lavyn

Loveable Christmas Angel: (4.6 out of 5 stars = 344 reviews)

"I loved My Cheeky Angel and His Devious Angel so I was excited to read this new "Angel" by Mimi Barbour. And I definitely wasn't disappointed. The romance wasn't the only touching relationship. And I admit I had a few tears and was choked up by the lovely ending. A beautiful story you're sure to enjoy."

Reviewed by ~ Hogwarts Wannabe

Dedication

*I'd like to dedicate this book to all my writing friends in
our local group WIP.
They've supported and encouraged me along the way
and I so appreciate all their help*

Also author of...

~*~*~*~

The Vicarage Bench Series
— Spirit Travel at its Best! —
She's Me (Book 1)
He's Her (Book 2)
We're One (Book 3)
Vicarage Bench Anthology (Book 4 – Books 1-3)
Together Again (Book 5)
Together for Christmas (Book 6)
Together Always (Book 7)

***

Angels with Attitude Series
— Angels Playing Cupid! —
The Angels with Attitudes Anthology (Books 1-3)
My Cheeky Angel (Book 1)
His Devious Angel (Book 2)
Loveable Christmas Angel (Book 3)

***

Elvis Series
— Make an Elvis Song a Book! —
She's Not You (Book 1)
Love Me Tender (Book 2)

***

Vegas Series
— Action–Packed Thrillers! —

Vegas Series – Complete Boxed Set
Partners (Book 1)
Roll the Dice (Book 2)
Vegas Shuffle (Book 3)
High Stakes Gamble (Book 4)
Spin the Wheel (Book 5)
Let it Ride (Book 6)
***

Undercover FBI Series
— Popular & Compelling! —
Special Agent Francesca (Book 1)
Special Agent Finnegan (Book 2)
Special Agent Maximilian (Book 3)
Special Agent Kandice (Book 4)
Special Agent Booker (Book 5)
***

Holiday Heartwarmers Trilogy
— Truly a Christmas favorite! —
Holiday Heartwarmers Series
Please Keep Me (Book 1)
Snow Pup (Book 2)
Find Me a Home (Book 3)
Frosty the Snowman (Book 4)
Love of my Life (Book 5)
***

Mob Tracker Series
— She's unstoppable! —
Sweet Retaliation (Book #1)
Sweet Justice (Book #2)
Sweet Resolution (Book #3

Sweet Endings – (Book #4)
Sweet Faith (Book #5)

***

Other Titles
I'm No Angel
Hotshot Cowboy
Big Girls Don't Cry
Christmas Runaway
The Surrogate's Secret
Mimi's Mix (Box Set)
'Tis the Season (Box Set)
Hearts, Flowers & Romance (Box Set)
Red Hot Divas (Box Set)
O authorsLove, Christmas (Multi-author Box Set)
Unforgettable Romances (Multi-author Box Set)
Kiss Me, Thrill Me (Multi-author Box Set)
Sweet and Sassy (Multi-author Box Set)
Unforgettable Heroes (Multi-author Box Set)
Sweet Heat (Multi-author Box Set)
Unforgettable Christmas (Multi-author Box Set)
A Christmas She'll Remember (Multi-author Box Set)
Snowflakes and Christmas Kisses (Multi-author Box Set)
Unforgettable Valentine (Multi-author Box Set)
A Valentine She'll Remember (Multi-author Box Set)

Unforgettable Suspense (Multi-author Box Set)
Unforgettable Danger (Multi-author Box Set)
Unforgettable Trouble (Multi-author Box Set)
Unforgettable Weddings (Multi-author Box Set)
A Wedding She'll Remember (Multi-author Box Set)
Enchanted Romances (Multi-author Box Set)
Sweet and Sassy Brides (Multi-author Box Set)

***

All Mimi's books can be found on her Amazon Author Page:
OR
Website: http://mimibarbour.com

Chapter 1

"Slow down, Mate! You could kill someone at this speed."

What the hell? Liam tramped on the brake and whipped his head around to stare in the back seat. There sat a stranger who looked rather pale, scrambling for his seat belt. "How did you get into my car?"

"Maybe you should watch the road instead of looking at me? I'm not about to hurt you, just a bloke along for the ride."

Liam wrenched the wheel and spun over to the curb, the screech of the tires attracting attention. Since he drove a convertible, and the hot sunny day had been perfect for putting the top down, he carefully controlled his voice. "Look, I don't know how the hell you got into my car or who you are, *Mate*," he said, "but you've got one minute to get lost, or I'll be forced to remove you. Trust me; it wouldn't be pleasant. I'd hurt you just because you've pissed me off, scaring the bejesus out of me."

"Jesus is on my side, I'm afraid. I'm sorry to have to tell you this, Liam. You could remove me, but I'd only return. You need me with you today."

Perplexed by the sincerity in his unwanted passenger's voice and by the fact that a stranger knew his name, Liam stopped raging. Searching for control, he took a couple of deep breaths, gritted his teeth and asked, "Why?"

"To stop you from killing someone."

"Okay, Bub! You're outta here." Furious at letting his guard down and getting played, Liam bolted from the front seat. He yanked open the back door, and motioned with his thumb.

"I'll only come back." The slim male with the dark hair and cynical attitude didn't move. Instead he crossed his arms and glared up at Liam. Familiar looking, he had Liam searching his brain for who he reminded him of. The pirate's jerkin, flowing white blousy shirt and tight leather pants were clues, but they didn't add up at first. It was the haircut that solidified his speculation. The guy looked enough like a young Johnny Depp to be his twin. Only his strong English accent didn't fit the picture.

"Stop playing silly buggers and get out of my car." Liam leaned in and his fingers met—air, because there was no one in his back seat. Stunned, he sagged against the side of the vehicle.

As if his intentions hadn't changed, his fingers continued reaching towards his hair, getting stuck in his wild mess. With a yank, he pushed them to the back of his head, interlocked his hands and studied the ground. Covertly, he peeked around him to see if anyone had noticed him talking to—what? A ghost?

He hadn't been drinking the previous evening. Deciding the time had come to cool it with the late nights; he'd turned off the idiot box at ten, after the football game, and for once had gotten to bed early. Actually managed to sleep for four consecutive hours before he woke and thrashed around until, luckily, he fell into another dreamless snooze for maybe an hour. Five hours altogether—unheard of for him. Therefore, he couldn't blame this lapse on being hung over or even on extreme tiredness. Blinking, he studied the back seat again. Still empty.

His cell phone rang, and he wiggled to free it from the pocket of his jeans. When he looked at call display, his eyes widened and he snorted. The word "Heaven" showed clearly on the screen.

What the...?

He pushed the talk button and held it to his ear. "Yeah?"

"Can I come back now?" The British accent from his recent guest was as clear as the headache starting to grind at the back of his head.

"I don't know who you are, or what your game is, but if you come anywhere near me, so help me God, I'll—"

"Ay, there, hang on. God is trying to help you. Just my bad luck that he sent me to carry out his wishes. Give over, would ya? I won't be in the way, I promise. I'll just ride along and maybe warn you to slow down from time to time. You drive like a maniac. You know that, don't you?"

Liam hit End and threw the phone into his front seat. First a quick glance in every direction, then he made his way around the car, got back behind the wheel and started the engine. With a squeal, he took off around the next corner, driving like a stuntman in a chase scene.

That's it! No more of those pills the doctor gave him. He'd rather have sleepless nights than daytime hallucinations. In a way, he'd be sorry to give them up. The last few times he'd resorted to using them, like last night for instance, they'd worked like a hot dam. No after-effects in the morning, and the horrific nightmares he normally suffered didn't appear at all. Not until a few minutes ago, that is.

What had the weirdo said? He worked for God? That's all he needed to complicate his life even further—a sidekick from the celestial universe. He checked the rear-view to be sure the invader hadn't re-appeared and then felt foolish. *Silly bugger's got you spooked!*

Around the next corner was a residential area where the speed limits dropped considerably. Keeping in mind the earlier warning, he lifted his foot from the gas pedal. Obviously, this wasn't enough for the vision now sitting next to him in the front passenger seat.

"Look 'ere chap. Kids live around here. Do us a favor then, and slow it down."

Liam gripped the wheel and only his eyes swiveled to look sideways. Yep, there he was again. Johnny Depp in his pirate costume. He decided not to acknowledge the hallucinatory poser, hoping he'd go away.

Teach him right for resorting to taking medication. Other than a night of drugged release, he'd known the underlying problem wouldn't be solved. And now look what he had to deal with—visions and voices. Damn doctors don't know diddly. Go in for tests, and all the quacks want him to do is see a shrink and spill his guts about his war experiences. Not gonna happen! Those days are over and reliving the horror is plain baloney—time to move on.

A flash in his peripheral vision attracted his attention. He snuck a peek sideways and Johnny sat, white-knuckling the front dash in an obvious hint—or a feeble attempt at humor.

"You can ignore me, but I'll not be going anywhere. I popped in to see you for a reason. And it's coming up shortly. So once again, Gov, for your own good, drive the speed limit."

"What are you? A ghost with a badge?" This time Liam glanced over and acknowledged his passenger just by talking with him.

"Nah, just an angel with a mission."

The light ahead turned yellow, and as was his habit, Liam speeded up in order to make the intersection before it turned red. The hiss from next to him made him laugh. "Relax, man. One thing I can do is drive. Anyway if you're an angel," he snorted while saying the word, "what do you care? You can't die again, can you?" All of a sudden, a slight pressure on the brake pedal effectively slowed the car, and it didn't come from him.

"Not worried about me. But you could hurt someone else. I'm here to make sure that doesn't happen. You couldn't live with another killing on your conscience."

Before Liam could suck up the words, a small child dashed into the road. Slow motion kicked in—as it was wont to do in such times—and his brain assimilated everything exactly as it was trained. From behind a parked car the toddler's ball had rolled from his reach. He'd chased it and ended up in front of Liam's bumper. Liam's quick reaction—slamming on the brake and wrenching the wheel—helped somewhat, but the saying, too little, too late, perfectly described the situation.

Chapter 2

"So how many dogs are you walking today, Sadie?" Her nosy but lovable neighbor liked to pull Sadie's chain about her livelihood. Not that she gave a hot damn. Sadie figured it was mostly envy that prompted the teasing. Greta's job as a hairdresser, a bitchy one at that, meant having to listen to her customer's complain about their lazy husbands and rotten kids all day, for which she had Sadie's total respect and sympathy.

"None. My next two days are free." Sadie leaned back in the bright red and yellow flower designed patio lounger with a sigh of utter contentment. While she'd been out watering her flower baskets, Greta had produced one of her special coffees with a wonderful smell and whipped cream and had cajoled her to sit for a few minutes

"Lucky dog! How will you survive without your

pooches?"

Sadie laughed at the pun, and then shook her head. "You make me sound obsessed. I love dogs. So sue me." Being a dog-walker was one of Sadie's three jobs. Many in the nearby high-class neighborhood fought over her services, and those she chose as clients were willing to pay top dollar.

"Uh-huh!" Greta smiled and crossed her arms, waiting.

"Whatever. I just hate to think of my charges not getting proper exercise because of their owner's lifestyles."

"You mean the lazy parasites who'd rather pay someone else to walk their dogs than get off their pampered behinds and do it themselves? Those clients?"

"Now, Greta. You're happy enough to take their money when you do their hair. So why would I begrudge them the opportunity to pay me to do something I love?"

"Well, when you put it that way... So what've you planned for all your free time?" The pseudo sarcastic way she asked the question made Sadie aware that she knew dam well there would be little free time.

Walking dogs wasn't her only responsibility. She also gave yoga classes five mornings a week, which left her afternoons free for the canine care. Then in the later part of the day, she gave free classes to the middle and high school students, tempting them to better themselves. She'd started helping out in the local school gym, and by getting to work with the overweight, unhappy kids, many times she'd convince them to give her workouts a try.

Also, she volunteered at the neighborhood care home a couple of evenings a week to work with the elderly, showing them that being sedentary might be easier and more comfortable, but in the long run, it's the wrong choice.

"Don't you have night classes tonight at Country Gate?"

"Usually I would, but they're having a dinner theatre evening specially set up for them by a group who's supposed to be brilliant. The old dears are so excited. Didn't you get a call to set up shop there to work your magic?"

"I couldn't go this time. We're booked solid, or should I say, *I'm* booked. But Julie will be there most of the day."

"You tease me about my good works, but my friend, you're also a softie and you know it."

"Maybe a bit soft-hearted, but you go as far as being soft-headed. Anyone can con you with a teary look and a sad story."

"Nah! I'm no one's sucker—trust me. But some people are just rather pathetic, and it's not a sin to give a helping hand now and again."

"Yeah! And again, and again, and—"

"Oh shut up." Sadie slugged the arm next to her

gently and grinned. "Gotta go for dinner to Mom's tonight. Wanna come?" The whining note made Greta laugh.

"I have no idea why you always want me to protect you from the mother you love more than—than is healthy. She just has to blink those false eyelashes of hers, and you roll over like that bizarre puffy poodle you walk. The one that prances around like some gay canine."

"Oh, you mean Giorgio? Hey don't make fun of the stud. He's very intelligent."

"He struts. Throws his head so all those silly pompoms bounce, and I swear he flirts with his eyes." Copycatting, Greta angled her pretty face to one side and fluttered her long dark eyelashes as if she were the dog. Sadie had to admit to there being a slight resemblance and laughed until she heard Greta's next sentence. "Sorry, kiddo, you're on your own with the tribe tonight."

Sadie's mother and two sisters meant the world to her. She loved them dearly and tried really hard not to give in to them every single time they set her up, but so far her record was lousy. Inwardly, she straightened her shoulders and stiffened her backbone. *Quit putting it off... beg... you know you will.*

"Awww! Don't make me face them alone. You never know what they'll talk me into."

"Sorry, friend. I have a hot date with the new customer, and he takes total precedence—even over one of your mom's meals."

"He must be absolutely gorgeous then."

"Oh, yeah!"

Sadie knew that Greta's biggest wish was to find someone to marry and raise kids with... preferably someone who would take her away from the business she professed to hate. Happy for her friend, Sadie reached over to squeeze her hand. She accepted that not everyone disliked the male species. And to be a good friend was to support another's right to be different.

But getting tied down and giving any man control over her choices—not in this lifetime. She glanced at her watch and jumped up, almost tripping on the silly fancy-dancy robe her mother had given her for Christmas. "Dam piece of silky... arrgg!" she muttered, then glared at Greta's "tsking".

With a final tug at the hem caught on a prickly branch, she said. "Here's hoping your date turns out to be better than mom's cooking. I'm off to get ready for my run. See you tomorrow to get the goods on the new dude."

Sadie stepped into her own condo, slid the patio doors shut and locked them. Their neighborhood here in DC, the country's capital, was pretty safe, but in this day and age anyone who didn't lock their doors was a flaming wheel-nut.

She returned the long-spouted watering can to the utility room—the one she'd used to water the frenzied mass of flowers on her patio and snatched her newest, just-washed yoga outfit to wear for her run because all her sweats were in the laundry basket. Another chore on her never-ending to-do list.

As she passed through to get to her bedroom, her eagle eye scanned the modern pale blue and green furnishings in her open-plan area and determined that her place was in its usual tidy state. Her bedroom only took a minute to organize, and while she straightened everything, she thought of how happy the uncluttered space made her feel and how glad she was that she'd held strong on her intention of moving from the family home.

It had taken a lot of guts for her to make the "It's time for me to move, Mommy" speech. Without Greta promising to protect her from the dangers her mother ranted about, she doubted if she'd have succeeded.

Hysterics from her mother and pleading from her sisters had all but broken her, but with the elbow periodically from her friend to strengthen her resolve, she'd held strong. Now, every day she took time to just "be in the moment" and feel the beautiful peace. I love it here, she thought, then danced a little jig. Love it, love it, love it!

In front of her mirror, she made sure that her black and turquoise stretch outfit fit properly—not too tight. She hated snug clothes that made her look fat. First she turned to the left, then the right, and picking up a small hand mirror, she checked the back. Tugging here and there, she finally gave up.

Grabbing at her soft hair, she tried unsuccessfully to clip it back. It was thick, naturally wavy, and Greta's pride and joy, so she couldn't cut it off as she'd constantly threatened. Finally, with some water, she managed to control it in a clip, and with a last perusal of her face, a dab of pink lip-gloss and pats on cheek for extra color, she grabbed her keys and made for the door.

Washington wasn't too hot for a change. Instead of the mugginess that hovered many times in this famous city, there was a cool breeze. The day was perfect for running. After a warm-up of stretches and bends, her body felt loose and lovely. She started out on her favorite route where, every once in a while, she'd see children playing in their yards—mostly with their overly protective parents watching.

Kids made her wish she liked the male species—at least enough to want to procreate with one. But during her torturous earlier years as a fat girl, it was the boys who teased her the worst, called her by the meanest names and made her want to crawl under the nearest rock. No, not a rock, she corrected the thought; make that a huge boulder.

Stop thinking about that garbage today... It's too beautiful. She shut down bad memories and got into her rhythm.

One moment she was ambling along at her unusual steady pace, in the next she registered the danger to a child chasing his ball into the street and somehow became magically jet-propelled. She never knew she could run so fast.

Immense satisfaction filled her for the split second she had him safe in her arms—before the impact. After the car hit her, the pain overrode everything—pain and shock.

Anger followed close behind. Rage at the pointlessness of the accident flooded into her scrambled brain and gave her the necessary courage not to pass out. Why some stupid fool had to show off his fancy wheels by driving like a lunatic, she'd never understand. Not only could she have been killed, but the child clutching at her might also have ended up a bloody corpse.

She hated to admit that some slick last-minute control on the driver's part had prevented them from even worse injury, but in her heart she knew it to be true. Nevertheless, he'd been well over the speed limit; therefore she felt justified in wanting to kill the SOB.

Just then, the boy's body jerked spasmodically, and she felt his terror. She needed to be strong. Keep him calm. Ignore the fire igniting into flames along her left side. She swallowed the blood that had pooled in her mouth from where she'd bitten her tongue and focused on keeping her voice from shaking.

Half lying, half sitting on the side of the road, she rocked her precious bundle back and forth and whispered, "It's okay, baby. I have you safe. We're fine."

From the end of a long tunnel, or so it seemed, she was aware that after the screech from the brakes stopped, a car door opened. But it wasn't until a large male rushed over and knelt beside her that she lost it.

Chapter 3

Oh god! A child! A massive adrenaline rush made breathing impossible and coherent thinking pure nonsense for Liam. Training and instinct took over.

Then just before the moment of impact, a smallish woman appeared from out of nowhere to lift the boy in her arms, swinging her back to the car to take the brunt of the blow. He'd never seen anyone move so fast—or so fluidly for that matter.

The sound of the car hitting her body tore his heart right out of him, leaving behind a gaping hole of anguished fear. Add the screech of the tires, and it would be a litany of sounds he'd never forget. Only one telling sob escaped as he bolted from the vehicle and slid to the ground next to the victims. Expecting blood and broken bodies, he wilted with relief when the mass of limbs unfolded and a very angry face pushed its way into his personal space until their noses all but came into contact.

Squeaking with fury, obviously unable to catch a full breath, the blonde doll glared and hissed like a cornered tomcat. And rightly so. He deserved whatever she could manage to push out from lips visibly trembling.

"Are you crazy? Driving—speeding lunatic—kill people."

"I'm so sorry." His hands reached to help.

Her visible effort to speak impressed the heck out of him. Finally she managed, "Get out of my way, you maniac." She slapped at his hands, all the while cuddling the quivering, shocked boy against her chest. Her trembling hand ruffled the boy's bangs and then checked his limbs. "Sweetie, are you okay. Are you hurt anywhere?"

"I want my mommy."

The wail almost broke Liam's heart. He answered in a voice softened by shame. "Of course you do, Streak. Don't cry, big guy. I'll get her for you. Where do you live?"

Just then a scream devastated what was left of his nerves as a woman heavy with child raced awkwardly towards them and collapsed to her knees. "Pedro!! *Mi niño*, are you okay? Are you hurt? Tell *mamá*."

Blondie released her hold on the boy, who was now angling and reaching in the direction of the distraught woman. "*Mamá*, I lost my ball."

"Don't worry, baby. I'll buy you another ball." While feverishly squeezing him to her, the mother rained kisses over the child's face and hair. "Just promise me to never run into the street like that again. Promise me." Saying those words seemed to ignite her anger, and her voice rose. She gripped the boy's arms and shook the sobbing, frightened child until Liam reached over and put his hands on top of hers.

"Don't," was all he said, but it was enough. Wails of fear and pain issued from between the mother's lips to harmonize with the child's as Liam wrapped his big arms around them both and hugged them back and forth before lifting them all up to their feet.

"We need to call an ambulance and take him to the hospital. A doctor should check him out, don't you think?" Liam insisted, and then hesitated when he felt the mother withdraw.

Blondie, still crouched on the ground, looked up at the mother and talked softly. "I'm sure the car didn't touch him, but we can't take any chances."

"I can drive him—" Liam broke in.

Blondie's head whipped his way. "Like that's going to happen. You shouldn't be allowed behind the wheel," she sneered.

"Right. Don't know what I was thinking. We'll call emergency. I'll get my cell phone right—"

"No." Pedro's mother broke into their conversation. "Pedro seems to be okay. He doesn't need to go to the hospital." Then she leaned over and her hand went to stroke the blonde's cheek for an instant as she looked into her eyes. "Maybe it's you who needs medical attention, miss? *Gracias—muchas gracias*. God will grace you for what you did today."

Blondie's hand covered hers. The two women shared an intimate look that spoke from one mother's heart to another woman's soul. A telling look that only women can share.

"I'm fine, just catching my breath." Blondie smiled and squeezed the other's hand.

Clutching the toddler, whose arms were wrapped tightly around her neck, the lady with the immense stomach turned clumsily in the direction of the curb and staggered forward. Her pregnancy looked to be advanced and the weight of the child seemed to be almost more than she could handle. But handle it she did. Stoically and slowly, she'd almost reached the sidewalk before Liam got a nudge from his irate victim, who slapped his leg, gave him "the look" and pointed.

Stunned, maybe, but not being too slow, he caught on and rushed over to help. "Ma'am, let me take the boy. He's too heavy for you."

The child peeked up at him from where he'd hidden his face on his mom's neck and wailed, "No." His arms tightened and he hugged even closer to his mother.

"No need, *señor*. Pedro is shy."

Driven, Liam couldn't let it go. "Look, ma'am, you need to take my card in case there're any problems that appear later, you know, if the boy needs to see the doctor, or for that matter, anything that might arise from this experience. I know the accident was my fault, and I want to take care of him."

"No, mister. It wasn't your fault. My Pedro ran in front of your car. That you stopped in time is a miracle, and the young lady who saved him is an angel. I'll say prayers for you both."

As if he didn't hear her, he put the card into the pocket of her sweater, forcing her to take it. "At least tell me your name and where you live, so I can check later to make sure he's okay."

"I'm Isobela Ruiz. We live in the white house, just here. Upstairs in the apartment." She nodded to the closest building, a dilapidated structure. Then she started forward again to where the stairs rose steeply.

He turned to go back to his car and began to hurry when he saw Blondie using the bumper to pull herself to her feet.

She rose slowly. White-faced, she leaned against the car.

"Help her, you idiot. She can't carry him up those stairs. She can barely walk herself."

Pivoting, he saw truth in her words. He sprinted back to Isobela and her son. "Let me take the boy and help you upstairs. It's too hard for you to carry him."

"*Mamá!*" The baby had a loud voice and a stubborn streak. "Again he tightened his hold around his mother's neck and hid his face in her hair.

"Thank you for offering. I'll just go slowly."

Liam didn't hesitate. "Pardon me, I *need* to help you." With those words, he gently lifted the pair in his arms and carried them up the crooked, badly chipped stairs to the top, where the flimsy screen door flapped in the wind. He set her down carefully and tousled the boy's hair, then turned in time to see that Blondie seemed to be in some difficulty.

Shit! His stomach tightened and gave him hell as he darted down the stairs to her side, just in time to catch her as she collapsed to her knees.

Chapter 4

She wrenched herself from the man's hands, then slapped at him when he wouldn't let go. "Don't touch me, you nutcase. Driving like you're racing in the frigging Indy 500." Her face ended up two inches from his. "Damn fool. You could have killed us."

He frowned, pulled back, and clenched his hands. "I'm sorry." What could he say? She was right, and he hated knowing it. On the other hand, he'd never shirked his responsibilities or hesitated to be accountable for his own actions. "I was speeding."

"Achh!" Disgustedly, she pushed him out of her space and again hung onto the car, trying to get the support she needed to rise.

"Don't be silly. Let me help you."

"No! I don't want you to touch me."

"Why are you being so stubborn? I just want to help." Without further ado, he lifted her into his arms, over the side of the convertible, and into the front seat.

"Are you crazy? Let me out of here. I'm not going anywhere with you. You all but killed me earlier with your stupid stunt, flying through the red light—"

"It was yellow."

"Was not."

"Was too." He glared at her over the side of the car and watched the sparks ignite in her cat-spitting green eyes. She crossed her arms and pushed her face closer. "Where do you think you're taking me?"

"To the nearest hospital."

"No way! I don't want to go to a hospital." A small dimple appeared on each side of her mouth as she ground her teeth.

"Tough! My car hit you. You need to see a doctor. With a slap on the door, he started around the front of the vehicle to get in at the driver's side.

"My mother's a nurse. She'll check me out. Just let me sit here for a minute, and then I'll be on my way. Hopefully never to run into you again."

"I think it was the other way around." *Have you lost your mind?* Whatever possessed him to make such a stupid joke about the accident? Obviously slipped out before his brain had caught up with his flapping mouth. *Adrenaline stimulation must have short-circuited your brain cells.*

His grin faded from the power of her direct, unflinching, not-amused stare.

"Look, it's the shock. I'm not usually so insensitive. Truly, I want to help, and if you let me drive you to your mother's, I promise not to go over thirty miles an hour." His hand began its rise, since he'd intended on putting it over his heart, but on second thought he decided to forgo the silly maneuver and hope the sincerity in his voice would be enough to convince her.

Her trembling fingers rose to secure her hair where it had escaped from a clip in the back, while her half-lidded gaze searched his face and contemplated. He saw her wince and reached to help with the silky strands. Her exclamation of annoyance stopped him immediately. A thought popped into his mind and wouldn't go away. She'd be officer material in any man's army; the rank of captain came to mind or maybe torturer, interviewer, person who extracts information.

As she lowered her arms, a groan escaped.

"That's it. You're hurt and being stubborn." He headed around to the driver's side and got into the car. He pushed the starter button, reached for his safety belt, and peeked to see what she thought about his high-handedness.

Yep, she wrenched at the door handle, fully intending to get out of his car. He reached past her and pulled it closed, then pushed the child safety locks and flinched when he heard her swear under her breath.

Green eyes blazed spikes of resentment aimed directly toward his face. "Get this into your head. I am not going anywhere with you. Not even to the corner. Now let me out of this car."

Without knowing why, Liam glanced into the rear-view mirror, not at all surprised to see his earlier phantom. Depp's look-alike radiated satisfaction in his raised eyebrows and smug smile. Pride flooded his face as he looked adoringly at the she-mule in the passenger seat.

"You're in for it now, my man!"

Liam had no idea how he could hear the voice, see the body and yet know with everything sane in him that he was arguing—mind-talking—with a ghost. *"Don't you start!"*

"Just saying. And I'm not a ghost."

"And I'm not your man." Should a ghost sound so huffy? Liam's daytime nightmare just ramped up.

He glanced at the girl next to him, who still had her arms crossed and her bottom lip protruding slightly from one of the prettiest shaped mouths he'd ever noticed. He'd seen similar on lipstick ads and had always wondered if they'd been surgically enhanced.

Somehow he just knew hers were nature's own creative perfection. As he watched, she sucked in the bottom one and chewed on it, a small tell that she was upset. It gave him confidence that maybe she wasn't as hard-assed as she'd been putting on. A throat clearing from behind pulled his thoughts back to the matter at hand.

"She won't listen to me. I can't force her."

"Give over, mate. She's hurt and not thinking clearly. Saw her life pass before her eyes, she did. You need to man up."

"Easy for you to say."

Liam caught her hand once again on the way up to fixing her hair. Short and curly, the blonde mass rioted around her small face, and no amount of tugging and twisting seemed able to control it, though she'd tried numerous times.

As soon as he touched her, she stopped the upward movement and fisted her fingers. From the steamy glare, he would have sworn her intentions had been to sock him in the chops.

"Calm down, honey. What can I do to make up for this? I've been trying to tell you how sorry I am. Please just let me get you to someone who can look after you."

Whether frustration or genuine caring seeped into his words, Liam wasn't sure—he didn't know what he felt. Angry at his own culpability? Thankful for not killing anyone? Accepting that he'd suffer more wakeful nights, new nightmares to add to the others, a sigh escaped that turned into a moan.

The noise got through to the she-tiger – sounds of a man in pain.

Chapter 5

Sadie clearly heard his pain. And it broke her reserve and stopped her from demanding that he call a taxi.

She searched his expression, and as hard as she found it to trust any man, she knew when a person was being honest. Her judge of character had been honed through years of suffering from her fellow humans' spiteful meanness and sad small minds. Boys, being the worst, had turned her off the male species to this day. Even at the age of twenty-eight, much to her family's horror, she hadn't changed.

And this guy personified the type of fellow she most detested, full of himself just because he'd been granted good looks and a tall strong body that moved like a sex advertisement.

She knew he waited for her to give in, and she never would have but for the agonized sound. It dug into her conscience and melted her resistance.

"Fine." She all but yelled the word. Pissed at herself for lacking the control to ignore his feelings, she wished the throbbing on her right side didn't hurt so badly. If she thought she could escape from his fancy silver metallic chick-magnet without collapsing in a heap of cuss words and whimpers, she'd be gone.

Blasted hair was driving her bonkers. She swiped it back from her face only to have it pool around her cheeks as soon as she moved her head. Shaving the mess looked more attractive every day.

Damn but she hated being at such a disadvantage.

"Well what are you waiting for, Gonzales?" Her tone lacked civility as she spit out the sarcastic nickname she'd tacked on at the end. Speedy might have worked better, but she didn't think he'd appreciate either one.

"Gonzales, like in Speedy? Not funny. My Name is Liam O'Brien. And I'm waiting for you to tell me where I should go."

"I'd love to tell you where to go—"

He chuckled, and the sound worked on her like honey in hot tea. "Okay, let me re-word that last phrase. Where can I take you?" He had warm brown eyes, and when they looked at a person, they smiled without his mouth moving. Not fair. Made him look likable. And he was an idiot.

She stiffened. Her bruised muscles screamed

with fury. Okay. Moving wasn't a good idea. Going home to her lonely apartment an even worse idea.

"I guess you'd better take me to my mother's place. She'll be thrilled to look after me." She couldn't hide her dismay at the thought of just how much her mother would be in her glory to have Sadie at her mercy. *It's going to be a long day.*

Bent over the steering wheel, Romeo started the car and pulled away from the curb with the utmost care, driving like the embodiment of a careful old man. Words escaped before she could stop them. Her darn temper wasn't safe at the best of times, and this had to be one of the worst. "Oh for Christ sake! We'll never get there at this rate."

He grinned into the rear-view mirror as if someone sat in the back seat. The guy was looney-tunes.

Leaning back, he relaxed and asked, "Where does Mom live?"

"A couple of streets over, on Mayfair. She's in the big white house on the corner, lots of windows, black shutters and ironwork around the window boxes."

"Are you sure I can't take you to the hospital first? I'm worried there might be internal damage. You seem pretty stiff and sore, and I saw you wince when you lifted your arm." He was worried; she heard it in his voice. Good! Silly bugger deserved to worry. He could have killed someone today.

"Just get me home," she growled. "My mother's

a nurse, a regular Florence Nightingale, and she'll like nothing better than to have one of her daughters to fuss over.

"You have sisters?"

"Two. You?"

"Only child."

"Figures!"

"Look lady, I'm trying to be a good guy here—to make up for earlier. Can't you meet me just a little bit of the way? I'm not even asking for half. Tell me your name at least. Unless you want me to keep calling you Crabby?"

"It's better than Honey. That's the house. Her car's in the driveway, so she's home. Just let me out here."

He ignored her and drove into the yard. "I'll help you."

"No. I can make it on my own." Sadie was glad she'd jogged in her new yoga pants and short stretch top to match. If she'd worn sweats like she did sometimes, there'd be underarm and chest stains and she'd have been mortified. She hated being at a disadvantage, even over something so stupid. Plus her mother would have commented and no doubt embarrassed her, which she often did without even realizing.

To Sadie's dismay, when she tried to move nothing worked. She'd stiffened like cold gravy. Using her hands, she lifted her right leg to angle it out of the car, and at the same time, she twisted her body, wanting to slide out. Except if she tried to stand, she'd fall flat on her face. And wouldn't that be cute. A guy who'd be perfect for the main part on *The Bachelor*, her mom's favorite show, the one Sadie thought pathetic, would watch her make a complete fool of herself.

"Hey you, don't be so stubborn. Sit there and don't move."

Like she could! Asshole acts like a trained soldier, she thought, watching him walk around to her side of the vehicle.

Ignoring her curt refusal, her knight stood with her door opened. He waited and watched, his hand lifting then stopping in mid-air as if he wasn't sure what to do.

"Oh for heaven's sake. Help me, you idiot. Can't you see I've stiffened up?"

"Sadie! What's happened?" Her beautiful flighty mother waddled towards the car, moving surprisingly fast for a woman her size. "What have you done to yourself this time?" Worry mixed with annoyance rang in her booming voice.

Sadie winced and then felt guilty for her feelings. She'd fought all her life to make the enormous love she had for her mother override her embarrassment at the way her mother looked, her big body, loud voice, and boisterous personality.

Red hair, obviously helped from a good dye job, backcombed and moussed to stick out every which way, seemed to send out sparks as she leaned over and stared into Sadie's eyes. The woman had magic at her disposal—the magic a mother had, which gave her a deep understanding of just what was going on in her daughter's head.

"You're hurt."

"A little."

She gently smacked Sadie's head. "Don't lie to your mother. What happened?"

For some strange reason Liam seemed to take umbrage at seeing her getting "what for" from her mom. Huffy with attitude, he intervened. "She ran in front of my car to save a little boy, and... Well, I hit her."

"With the car?"

Sadie shook her head at her mother's dumb question. "Yes, Mom, with the car. But the child's fine."

"I'm glad. But you're not. You need to come into the house so I can check you out. And don't argue." She held up her hand in front of Sadie, effectively stopping her from uttering any opposition, which she had no intention of doing. A tweak of conscience reminded her of the particulars in their relationship. For instance, since she always argued, the poor woman was just playing by the rules.

"I'll carry her." Liam stepped around the large woman and bent with his arms reaching. "I wanted to take her to the hospital but she refused."

"Of course she did. One tough chick, my girl.

Just like her jackass-stubborn father, and I mean that in the best way, God bless his soul and keep him smiling."

Sadie felt herself being lifted as if she weighed nothing. She'd instinctively tried to lighten his load by making her body as small as possible.

This is torture, she thought, feeling his hands in places they didn't belong. Being held this close to a man scented with one of those just-for-men colognes, I feel like a silly heroine in the movies. Teach him right if he hurts his back. The thought popped in and made her stomach tighten.

Every morning, she stood in front of her mirrored closets and angled every which way to see the body she'd yearned for all her life. But it was as if the chubby girl she'd worked so hard to get rid of still hovered inside.

Realistically, she knew it wasn't so. She knew that all her running and yoga classes had given her a slim and healthy form. Her eyes confirmed it each time she gazed in a mirror, or into every store window, or, truth be told, any reflective surface, actually.

Swinging above the ground, securely cuddled, Sadie came back to earth. While her mother bustled along, nattering to Sadie's cheerful carrier, she kept her arms crossed and glared at the both of them.

Trust her mom to take a shining to this Liam guy. Knowing the woman had eyes like a hawk, no doubt she'd registered the make and model of the convertible down to the total package price, inventoried his clothes and knew what designer names, if any, were on the labels, and could draw a police composite of his features.

From his overly long wavy hair and eyebrows that formed the perfect shape to hood his wickedly dangerous smiling eyes to the upward curving lips that smiled too sarcastically, sure as hell her sharp-eyed parent had catalogued it all.

Sadie wished she'd never run into him. *Hold it! He'd run into her.* She smirked at her own silliness. Still, if she had her druthers, they'd never have met. Seeing how palsy-walsy her dear, nosy mom was behaving, he'd undoubtedly be invited to dinner to see if one of her sisters could pick up a husband. Why did this have to happen to her?

A picture of little Pedro drifted into her mind. Black curls rioting around his baby face, while his chubby little legs pumped hard, trying to catch up with his toy. How could she have stood by to watch the little angel battered, maybe killed?

That the fool driving had such quick reflexes was a giant plus. A bonus she hadn't counted on because there had been no time. One second she was going to cut across the street, and the next she had the kid in her arms while flying through the air.

If he'd hit them dead on—okay not the best wording—they'd have been toast. But he'd swerved and reduced the impact, saved them from serious injuries. Well he wouldn't get any commendations from her. The whack-job had still been driving too fast.

Her rioting thoughts ramped up her dreadful headache, and she knew from the frown her mother shot in her direction that she probably looked mean. But she didn't give a rat's ass. Today had been her day to play, and now she'd be stuck here for who knew how long.

She stared her mother down for a few seconds and then felt her satisfaction waver and completely fade when her mom winked and blew her a kiss. Darn woman never failed to penetrate guards no one else could.

"Just put her here in the living room on the sofa." Liam lowered her gently and stayed bent over to push her mop away from her forehead.

"There's a bruise here. You hit your head?"

"Pedro and I bumped, that's all." She wrenched away from him too quickly and couldn't stop the cry of pain.

He straightened and turned to Sadie's mom.

"Is she always so disagreeable?"

"Yep! That's my girl!" Her mom's sideways smirk, nod, and snort didn't make her feel any better. "On the other hand, you'll never meet anyone with a bigger, more loving heart."

"Beatrice!" Sadie's glare and icy tone constituted a warning most wouldn't ignore.

"Sadie girl, you call me that again, and I'll call you-know-who and tell him you didn't mean to be rude, and you'd really like him to bring his dog back."

"Sorry, Mom." Sadie smiled, knowing it was nothing but a sick imitation, but her mother seemed to accept it and nodded. After all, she did deserve the rebuke.

She knew how much her mother hated her full name. But she also knew her dear bratty mom understood that if Bubba Jones ever came within ten feet of her again, she'd take a chop-saw to the numbskull. Imagine, feeding a Shiatsu chicken bones every day and then blaming the poor dog's condition on her running the animal too hard. Cheap bastard still hadn't repaid her for the vet bills after Sadie had realized the dog suffered and had taken her in. Aggrr. Just thinking about him had her visualizing chains and a horsewhip.

"By the way, as you've probably figured, I'm Sadie's unfortunate mother, Bea Bertolli. Years ago, I worked as a nurse. I'm sure she told you that so you'd bring her here rather than a hospital."

"She insisted." Liam actually sounded hard done by.

Hey, what am I? Invisible? They spoke about her like she wasn't even in the room. Irritation joined the other sensations she suffered, like anger, discomfort and frustration. And that made her feel even more like ripping the heads off the carnations arranged in front of her on the coffee table.

"Look, Liam, I'd like to give her the once over to make sure she's just bruised, so if you wouldn't mind zipping into the kitchen and getting yourself a cold drink, it won't take too long."

"Mom, I'm sure Mr. O'Brien—"

"Call me Liam." He shook her mother's hand and turned on the charm, grinning as if she were a groupie and he a football star.

Sadie could feel her pissed-off-ed-ness rise to a whole new level. "I'm sure Mr. O'Brien has things to do." So she spoke a bit too loud. She flipped her hair out of her eyes and glared her challenge. "You should be on your way." This time she lowered the volume.

"Nonsense!" Bea took charge.

Liam started out by shaking his head up and down at her words and ended up shaking it back and forth in her mom's direction. If he was trying to be funny, she didn't appreciate his sense of fun as much as her mom, who laughed and patted his arm, then pushed him in the direction of the kitchen.

"Go through this door and down the hall. Make yourself at home by the pool. You'll see the patio from in there. I'm thinking this girl will need a nice hot-tub soak, and it would help for you to carry her there."

"No problem," said Liam. "I'll wait for your call."

Sadie watched his butt action as he strode from

the room and couldn't stop the grin when she heard a huge sigh she knew her mother intended for her to hear.

"You're incorrigible." Even though she'd tried to maintain a straight face, her lips had turned upward of their own accord. Being serious was impossible around Bea, who she adored. Of course, it didn't stop her from rolling her eyes and shaking her head at her naughty parent's shenanigans.

"Come to my bedroom and you can change into a swimsuit in there. I'll help support you unless you'd like me to call your young man?"

"Stop it. You're not funny."

"Tsk, tsk. Baby, you're grumpy for a reason, so I'll forgive you. Even as a child, when you suffered any discomfort, you were a pain in the ass. Nurse's advice... I'm going to get you some Tylenol, then a long hot soak and a good massage, and you'll feel ten times better. "

A dozen or so agonizing steps later, clinging to her mom's arm, Sadie carefully lowered her butt onto the bed. Her mother undressed her and gasped when she saw the swelling black and blue bruise forming from her hip, along her back, and—the worst area—her shoulder.

Bea's tender ministrations while searching for broken bones was done quickly and efficiently. From a doctor's bag, she produced a stethoscope and examined Sadie's blood pressure. Then she felt around the lump on her forehead and searched her skull for others. An examination of her eyes and a check of her blood pressure had her sighing with relief. Once satisfied that Sadie's injuries involved only superficial damage, Bea settled down.

"I'll get you a suit, honey." She kissed Sadie's head wound very gently and left the room returning in a few seconds. For such a large woman, she moved fast when she had good reason. Sadie recognized the garment as soon her mother appeared with it in her hands. And the daring glare she saw from the other woman had her biting her lip and shutting her mouth.

Black, cut low in front, backless to her waist with see-through netting across her chest, it wasn't a style she'd normally be caught dead wearing. But her mother loved to shop for her girls and, rather than cause hurt feelings, Sadie had worn it a few times when only the family, which consisted of her two younger, unmarried sisters and her mother, were home.

Carefully and with help, she slid on the bathing suit, each movement awkward and painful, like there were hot fingers inside her body squeezing all the muscles, wrenching and twisting.

"Oh, no, you don't!" Before Bea could move to open the door, Sadie grabbed her arm. "Give me a robe. I'm not going anywhere like this."

Bea twirled and reached for the muumuu she loved wearing. She'd left it draped over her chair, and it was in easy reach. A silky green shapeless tent that surprisingly fit any size and draped the body wearing it. Before Sadie could refuse, Bea had lifted it over her head and arranged it to fall gracefully to the floor. Since Bea stood a few inches taller, it reached Sadie's ankles and floated around her as she stubbornly lurched towards the door.

Chapter 6

Liam grabbed a cola from the refrigerator and surveyed his surroundings. The kitchen was a mixture of very modern versus old country. The gigantic wooden table in the middle of the room held a huge grinning ceramic pig painted in a variety of brilliant colors and wearing an endearingly goofy expression. There were fresh green herbs that looked like parsley planted in its open back.

In the actual cooking area, the appliances were chrome and huge with a center island that any cook would envy. A bay window full of colorful ceramic pots of basil, mint, and chives caught his attention, and he instantly thought how his father would love this bright, sunny room.

Liam wandered over to the French windows at the other end of the room, and the paradise outside had him reaching for the handle. As soon as he stepped out the door, a medium-sized hound glanced up with one blood-shot eye as it lay, spread-eagled, in front of a fancy doghouse. It started to bark but gave up half-way through so it just sounded like an exclamation.

His first reaction was to leave the mutt alone, but the dog's expression of friendliness overrode it. He bent over to pet the lazy canine. "Hey tiger, I'm a friend." Speaking low in a soothing tone did the trick. The dumb mutt sat up crookedly on its haunches, back legs comically spread, and panted—the tail wagging from side to side like a mechanical rope. Liam could have sworn the critter grinned, its half-hidden eyes twinkling like a human's.

Ruffling folds of fur with an extra caress for the pendulous silky ears, Liam made a lifelong friend. He stood, intending to move farther into the garden paradise. As if it needed to impress, the young dog stood up and wiggled from side to side. "What have you got to be so happy about?"

A barking growl answered his question, and he laughed. Damn dog was almost human. Liam spotted a ball, picked it up, and threw. A splash followed, and he realized he'd lobbed it into the pool. Without hesitation the dog loped and leapt—a huge splash the result.

"I see you've found Susie's weakness. Never knew a dog that loved to swim like mine. She's been a water baby since a puppy, probably a good thing, since she has a tendency to be a bit odoriferous and bathing her is a nightmare." Bea talked as she guided Sadie toward the far end of the path.

Liam watched the two women make their way through the garden. One moved fluidly, her weight not a hindrance at all. The other limped, winced, and muttered.

Sadie unknowingly stopped in a spot where the sun framed her from behind. Outlined seductively through the gauzy material of the dress the wind molded around every luscious curve, her body would fuel any hot-blooded man's fantasy.

Gorgeous, a crowning glory of gold—a nebula of curls flittered around her head and caught his mesmerized gaze. He wished he had the right to approach her and smooth them back as he stole a kiss.

What the hell am I thinking? He started the lecture that normally worked to stop his interest in any female from getting out of control. And this time he had help.

"Bless my soul. For a bloke who can't sleep, or work, or even relate to his own father..."

Liam knew that voice. He turned a complete circle and, sure enough, there was his imaginary friend, or whatever he was, leaning against the wall of a small ivy-covered hut, tapping his toe and looking annoyed.

"I don't know how to be friends with girls."

"Rubbish! You treat them the same way you do the guys on your team, with respect."

"Liam." Bea snagged his attention. With a warning note ringing in her loud voice, she nodded her head in Sadie's direction. "As much as my bratty daughter will try to refuse your help, she needs to get into the hot tub sometime soon."

Both turned to see Sadie stagger towards the steps, stop and cling to the railing, and moan involuntarily. Face white, jaw clenched, the muscles in her well-formed arms bulging, she strained to hold herself upright. Just in time, Liam reached her as she started to weave. Whipping her into his arms became a battle of wills as she stiffened and pushed herself away from his chest.

"Would you stop manhandling me? I just wanted to sit for a minute."

"You mean you were going to land on your ass, maybe hurt yourself worse."

Bea reached them and, with a not-so-tender pat against her daughter's cheek, settled the issue.

"If you don't behave and let Liam help you, I'll get him to take you to emergency, and I'll sign your mulish butt in there myself. You know I can't take the heat in that tub, so I can't go in with you, but if Liam doesn't mind, I'll sit with you while he checks out the change room for a pair of trunks and then he can babysit you—"

"Not a chance in hell."

"You're not going in there alone, especially after the pills I gave you. Besides, I'm really not a hundred percent certain about you not having a concussion. You need someone close by in case there's a delayed reaction to the accident. Meantime, I'll get lunch started. The girls will be home soon."

Liam ignored Sadie's frustrated sigh and set her down like a collector would handle precious china. Then he moved to do Bea's bidding.

He supposed it was the least he could do, staying with her in the water and keeping her safe. After all, it was his stupidity and carelessness that put her in this devastating state.

His interest in the little firebrand increased every time he laid eyes on her. She made his blood pump at such an alarming speed it left his heart racing and his mouth drier than the plains in the thirties.

He grinned coldly when warnings bombarded and wouldn't be shut down. *So who's going to keep her safe from you?*

As soon as he'd shut the door to the change room, Liam reacted. He swung around, waiting for his shadow to appear, and sure enough, there he was. Medium build, wearing his gay pirate's outfit and the famous grin the actor used so convincingly.

"What the hell do you want from me?"

"I want you to leave her alone. She's delicate and you like to break things."

"Look, I'm not interested in women right now. I have a lot on my plate. But I can't ignore the fact that I almost killed her today, now can I? If her mother asks me to help, then, buddy, you better believe that's exactly what I'm going to do."

"You didn't kill her because I stopped you. And, *buddy*, women have always flocked around you like you were chocolate, but this girl's different. She has no ammunition against your experience."

"I beg to differ. She's shot me down at every turn." The droll note in Liam's voice made the angel smile happily.

"I should think so. She sees right through ya, she does."

"Then go away and let me do what I have to do."

"And that be..."

"I'll help her in the hot tub, and then leave." Liam blinked and the spirit disappeared—poof, gone! Except for his parting shot that echoed in the small room:

"Just be sure that you do. The less time she spends around a bounder like you, the better."

***

Both women's eyes widened when he returned dressed in the only choice of bathing suit that would suffice—a cargo camouflage style that, no matter how tight he tied the strings, hung low on his hips. Their stares made him uncomfortable, especially when he realized he'd pulled in his gut and tightened his chest muscles.

"*Do us a favor then, Stud. Don't let it swell your head.*" So, his ghoulish friend hadn't left after all, probably just hovered around, spying like some otherworldly peeping tom.

"*Sticks and stones...*"

Liam answered. "*You can do me a favor and go... away!*" The spook's laugh faded, then disappeared.

Bea whistled softly and caught his attention. Stares always followed him whenever he bared his toned and tanned body. Usually it annoyed, but today he felt kinda flattered until Sadie's words left him rather deflated.

Sadie slipped off her cover-up clumsily and then said, "Are you waiting for a drum roll?"

He used the same smart-ass, one-sided grimace that shut-up the guys in his troop when they gave him the gears, lifted her up in his arms, and strode up the steps, intending to gently lower her into the bubbles.

Instead, an outside force gripped him, and before he knew it, he'd dumped her in without any warning.

Once she surfaced and wriggled to a seat as far away from him as possible, she gripped her dripping hair to push it back behind her ears and made as if to rise. Except that the awesomeness of the heated water registered. A look of bliss replaced the glare of anger.

"Oh, Lordy, Lordy, Lordy. This is heaven."

With great care not to get in her path, Liam

stepped into the tub and took the seat farthest from where she lounged and closest to the steps for escape. He heard Bea chuckling in the distance and watched as she disappeared into the house.

A few minutes of silence followed as Liam observed Sadie stretch and exercise her neck and shoulders very slowly, careful not to be too extreme in her movements.

It was like watching a sleek cat perform her ablutions. He found himself fantasizing her licking her skin like a puss would it's fur, and then thanked all that was decent for the bubbling water that hid his unexpected erection.

All of a sudden, music could be heard from near-by speakers, and a good old country-and-western song wailed out in a woman's marvelous twang. The words made him smile and look around. He knew who'd helped Bea make the song choice. "Heaven's just a sin away-y-yy."

Not so Sadie. Her head dropped to her chest, her eyes closed comically and then he heard what she'd obviously known to expect.

Worse than the caterwauling of a female cat being overpowered by a determined male suitor, the voice that sang along to the words grated on every functioning nerve end.

Amazement he couldn't begin to hide had to be plastered all over his face.

"Doesn't it hurt?" he asked.

"You have no idea!"

"I meant her throat."

"What can I say? She loves to sing."

"And you love her."

Silence reigned as she tried to ignore his comment. But he kept staring, fully intending for her not to look away. His S.W.A.T. training gave him the edge, and it worked. Mesmerized, she stared back, and finally a small grin appeared.

"Yeah! I love her."

Saints be praised. The first genuine smile he'd seen on her face was a lovely sight to behold. Already beautiful, she rose up the scale way past ten, right to infinity.

Vying for his attention, his body's swelling became enormously uncomfortable. He perused the multi-flowering bushes, the patio lanterns entwined with twinkle lights barely visible and even the red roof tiles. Anything to keep his mind off the woman lounging across from him, the woman whose internal magnet drew at the one pitifully whining in his own body.

Finally the song ended and wonderful silence wrapped around them in their private little world. With a sigh, Sadie leaned her head back and relaxed.

Liam let her enjoy the quiet while he enjoyed her enjoying the quiet. A splash in the pool caught his attention.

Susie, the Bloodhound, was swimming in a straight line from one end of the pool to the other.

Liam watched, and it soon became apparent, the wacky animal was doing laps. He chuckled.

"It's how she exercises. Bloodhounds are notoriously lazy dogs, so this is quite unusual. Once Mom realized how much Susie loves the water, she trained her to do laps. Two or three times a day, the dog ends up in the pool. She likes it best to have someone with her. Then she really performs."

"This is eye-opening. I've always thought people had to walk or run their dogs to give them exercise."

"Susie suffers through walks three times a week with a dog walker, who I'm happy to say isn't due for two days."

His quizzical frown must have registered, because before he could even form the question, she answered. "I'm the dog walker."

Chapter 7

The words didn't register at first. The quiet had lulled her while she let the pulsating heat and heavenly water work its magic. Even having to share the tub with Liam stopped bothering her once she understood he wasn't going to try chatting her up.

Then it hit her. For the first time since the accident, Sadie recognized what a pickle she was in. She realized she had a lot of phone calls to make and some explaining to do if she couldn't carry on with her regular routine. Wait, she thought, I can still lead the yoga classes, just have to hold off on the extreme moves for a while.

Walking the dogs, well, that was another matter. Every afternoon during the week, she had six dogs on each of her three runs to exercise.

The first batch, the smallest group, she picked

up at the local SPCA, and that wasn't a problem because she could take them to the nearby yard and let them run or, if she wasn't available, there were other volunteers to take over.

It was the hoity-toitys' pets that required more of her time and stamina. Eight frisky dogs whose rich owners paid her top dollar to be responsible for their daily workout. To pick them up in her van, get them to the park, walk and run the scheduled two miles and deliver them all back home in an hour and a half required vigilant clock watching and a whole lot of patience.

Those animals weren't your run-of-the-mill, happy-go-lucky, glad-to-see-you kind of dogs. Many expected to be carried. Others pulled and tugged on their leashes, stubbornly trying to wield control. Still others, the shit disturbers Sadie called them, purposely ran back and forth getting the leads twisted, acting ornery, growling, biting at each other until separated.

But over time Sadie knew she'd worked wonders. Most of them had settled into their routines and even looked happy to see her now, rather than running to hide or flatly refusing to move.

Now what'll I do? It had taken her many months of hard work to get to this comfortable zone. It could all be undone in a matter of days with the wrong person to replace her. If she only had to walk, it might be doable, but the way she felt right now, managing and controlling those dogs would be impossible. Alone, anyway.

"Something's bothering you. I can see by the changing expressions on your face." Liam's soft voice interrupted her worrying.

"No. Nothing's wrong."

"Hell it's not."

Sadie decided, since he asked, she'd hit him with truth. "Here's the thing. I can't be laid up right now. I need to work..." She stopped talking when he frowned.

"Don't ask if you don't want to know." Sarcasm ripped through the words.

"Hey, settle down, Miss Doomsday. I'll be happy to reimburse your wages during this time—"

"I don't need or want your money, Hotshot." She lowered her voice once she heard herself yelling. "I need someone reliable to replace me for the days I can't do the job." Sarcastically she added, never expecting he might agree, "So if you want to walk my canines, you might be of some help. Otherwise..." She didn't say the words, but the smirk she glared at him was more than adequate to let him know her thoughts.

"I'll do it." The plus side was that he hadn't hesitated. The minus was that he'd offered, and she was tempted.

"Give me a break. I'm serious."

"So am I. Look, I might not have a great reputation as a driver, but I assure you, not only can I walk, I've been doing it with no problems to speak of since I was a year old."

Sadie's stomach somersaulted. Warnings went off in her head like church bells ringing in the New Year. *That man's smile is lethal,* she thought. *How can I spend the next few days near this charmer—yet how can I not?* On the weekends, she'd have had all kinds of help. But during the week, it would be nigh on impossible to find someone with two days open.

"What about your own work? How can you take the time off?"

"I'm between posts right now. I've finished my stint in Iraq, and not sure if I want to sign up for another placement. Still have a few weeks to think on it. So, I'm free and all yours."

Not even tempted, you cheeky bugger! The thought popped into Sadie's head and wouldn't be dismissed.

"If you don't want him, can I have him?" Her sister Dora arrived just then. Her voice actually whined with desire. "Pretty please?"

"Settle down, Sis. He's not mine to give. But I can introduce you. Liam, this tease is my oldest sister Dora." Sadie pointed to a large-sized girl who now had her pretty face propped up on her hands as she leaned against the side of the tub, eating up the gorgeous male with her hot gaze. "This is Liam. As long as you never get near his car, he's probably harmless."

Liam shot her a sly grin, and without intending to, she returned it. *Don't go there, girl! He's too much man for you.* There's that warning voice again. That's all she needed—to start hearing things.

Dora looked wickedly curious. "So what did he do to you in his car?"

Realizing how her sentence had sounded to her sister, she tried to back up, but it was too late. Now she understood the naughty grin. How the hell did she get herself into these fixes?

Liam cut in before she could answer. "I accidentally hit her with it."

Dora jokingly backed away and held up both hands. "He's all yours, Sadie. I like 'em rough, but that's a wee bit mean, even for me."

Just then Bea and another female wandered up to stand beside Dora. The three women were all the same size; the two were younger replicas of their mother.

Sadie often wondered if she was actually related to the other three females in her family. Every one of them was large, happy-go-lucky, and beautiful in her self-confidence. Whereas all Sadie's life, she'd detested her chubbiness. From the moment she'd left home, the overweight girl had worked hard to be the size she'd always dreamed of being.

She'd planned her meals around a sensible eating plan. And exercise not only became her way of life, it became the means for her to make a living.

"Liam," said Bea, pointing at the giantess beside

her. "This is Sadie's sister Maggie, our brilliant financier who manages the family business."

Sadie saw him look somewhat bemused by the three strikingly attractive, full-bodied women who surrounded his side of the tub. She knew what a force her family was and how overwhelmed they made one feel by their dramatic presence. Heck, when the Bertolli females actively worked at being overpowering, awesome didn't even come close to describing their compelling attraction.

Liam, looking a bit stunned, whispered to her in a voice everyone heard. "I think I need to get in touch with my feminine side."

The boisterous laughter fueled by his remark made Sadie flinch. Too loud, too rough, too happy... just too much. Secretly, her family had mortified Sadie for as long as she could remember, and hiding her feelings from them had become a daily Oscar-winning performance.

Her friend Greta, after one wine-drinking, soul-sharing night of confessions, came to a conclusion that made the most sense. As much as Sadie loved them, they embarrassed her. To compensate, she gave in to them every time—except for once. She'd moved out and saved her soul.

Maggie's smile faded first, and then she leveled him with the old gimlet-eye Maggie-stare that had most people, men even more so, slinking for cover.

Sadie watched as Liam not only returned the look but had the audacity to wink. Oh-oh! Sadie thought. My friend—you're a goner.

Except that Maggie surprised her by winking back and saying. "Wanna join us for a barbecue, Gorgeous? I can promise such good food, you'll think you'd died and gone to Iron Chef Heaven."

Sadie secretly appreciated that Liam first glanced her way, eyebrow raised, silently asking for permission before accepting. Pretty classy for such a speed demon.

Not wanting to seem too eager for his company, because she wasn't—really—she shrugged her best "who cares," turned away, then listened while holding her breath.

"Might not be a good idea, honey. Sadie is pretty annoyed with me, and with good cause. I wouldn't want to overstay my welcome." With the water sluicing his muscular frame as he rose, he sloshed over to her and knelt closer. "I'm a hungry guy and the smells coming from the house have been driving me nuts, but say the word and I'll leave."

Dora and Maggie's audible unison sighs let her know where their preferences lay. And the fact that Bea hadn't yet overridden her even having a choice was perplexing. Given authority in a group who usually never acknowledged that she had a vote, made her feel stunned. This power could be addictive.

She looked from one to the other and old habits kicked in. "Sure. Stay if you want to." Then she topped off her capitulation with a big fat lie.

"Makes no difference to me."

Chapter 8

Bea overrode Sadie. "You need to take Liam up on his offer and stop being so bullheaded. Do you have someone else you can hire to walk the dogs at such short notice?"

Dora cut in. "Sadie, you know those folks expect to get their money's worth when they pay top dollar for a service. You've taken on the responsibility of looking after their animals, and they'll assume that either you'll do the job or you'll have help. I work with them every day, and I know how they think."

Liam looked around the food-laden table. The wonderful smell of barbecued ribs was only exceeded by the taste. Corn on the cob, baked potatoes, sweet-and-sour meatballs, salads, and homemade buns had been piled on his plate with never a thought of asking him his preference—which, by the way, wasn't a problem. Best meal he'd had in ages.

Listening to the women conversing, he relaxed and decided he didn't need to be his own advocate when he had Sadie's family. Whether or not he should have offered, he didn't really know, especially since he'd clearly heard the shouted *"Hang on!"* in his head. All he did know was that her dilemma was his fault and, truth to tell, the longer he could put off dealing with his own shit the happier he'd be.

Once he zoomed back into the heated argument surrounding him, he could see that Sadie had lost the battle. Poor little doll looked whipped, and his conscience kicked in big time.

"If Sadie would rather work with someone else, that's not a problem." He smiled at her to let her see his sincerity. And he liked that she smiled back, a small tug at her pretty lips with their curled-up edges, but nevertheless a smile.

Bea spoke before the others could. "She has no one else. I'm not sure if you're aware, but our family own a business called 'Angels' and we do home care for the infirm, the elderly, and the rich who can afford to have someone come to their homes and look after them. We employ a number of women who like to look after folks—retired nurses, caregivers, and so on. But early in the program, we realized that many of these people had animals they cared about, especially dogs that needed to be exercised every day.

"Sadie thought up a plan where she was in charge of this part of the business. And it's worked out very well. We're all happy with her role both as the dog walker and the fitness trainer. She also does yoga with many of the clients. However, this keeps her very busy, and we've been telling her for some time to slow down. Except as you might have noticed, she's as stubborn as her jackass mule-headed father, God bless his soul and keep him smiling."

Mama Bertolli tickled his funny bone. He smiled, and then a mushy feeling exploded when she returned it so sweetly. The thought he'd had returned, and he said, "Couldn't the dogs miss a couple of days? It *is* an emergency. It's not like she's at fault for the accident."

"It's a business, Liam. They would expect us to be prepared. I've been after Sadie for some time to take on a partner to train with the animals. We're talking spoiled canines that many of these people treat like precious babies. They have idiosyncrasies that need to be understood."

"The dogs or the owners?" Liam grinned at the thought.

Bea's face stayed serious even if her eyes twinkled. "Both. And Sadie has their number."

"The dogs or the owners?" He couldn't help himself.

"Both." This time she did laugh.

Dora piped in as if she'd stayed quiet long enough. "Sadie, take Liam up on his offer. He's a big guy and those mutts won't scare him. You know you need someone who can take control."

Liam raised his eyebrow at Sadie, wondering what the hell he'd gotten himself into. This time her grin evoked pure mischief.

Chapter 9

Later that day, Liam drove through his familiar childhood neighborhood where he'd ridden his first bike—his father running behind him holding on to the seat. He'd forgotten that memory until his phantom friend all of a sudden appeared as his passenger and mentioned it.

"How did you know?" Liam was shocked. He pulled over to the curb a few houses before his own and parked the convertible.

Johnny, Liam's nickname for the ghost dude, gave him the "what-are-you-stupid?" look, and he felt his bile rising. Man, he wished a guy could punch out an angel.

Ignoring his celestial stalker, he turned away to watch as his old man, hunched over a little more with age, raked the leaves, and another vision blasted from his memory banks. Him and his dad making a big pile, and then him running and leaping, leaves flying in every direction, his father doubled over with laughter.

Unfortunately, his thoughts didn't stop there. He remembered his mother at the window flaying them both, especially her husband. With an ugly sneer on her face, she'd cut him down, the words vitriolic and hurtful—the old man taking it, saying nothing. Sorrowfully, reaching to help him out of the mess, his dad had returned to work, head lowered and peace was restored.

Anger seized and tightened his gut to where he had difficulty breathing. He remembered that it had always been that way; his mom berating her husband, and the man allowing her to cut him up in little pieces. Liam had hated it, and as he'd gotten older, he'd begun to hate his father for allowing his wife such wicked control. Sick inside from remembering, he started the car and peeled away, tires squealing.

Once past the old place, he checked the rearview mirror and watched his father stop what he was doing and examine the passing vehicle. In seconds, Liam saw his shoulders stoop worse than ever, a riveting visual of misery and despondency.

"You couldn't cut him some slack, hey? Had to make sure he saw you, dig the knife in a little deeper?" The angel sounded sad.

"*What's it to you?*" Liam had to grate his teeth to stop the sob that almost escaped. He crunched his lips together so they wouldn't wobble; he was that close to losing it. What the hell was wrong with him? Ever since that last patrol, he'd felt vulnerable and weak. As a man who'd never let himself be anything but strong and cocky, he didn't have a clue how to handle this bullshit.

After the last horrific battle, he'd gone through intense debriefing, but it hadn't worked for him, not this time. Maybe if he'd stayed longer, he'd have dealt with the psychological stress, but his time had run out. He'd been sent home with a Distinguished Service Cross in one hand and his broken spirit in the other.

Now he had two choices for his future. Take on a new career. Or sign up again. With his unique capabilities as an elite member of Special Forces, he had his choice of missions both here and overseas.

"Aye there, you don't have to make up your mind just yet, you know. You have time." The British accent soothed, stroking his anxiety to where it magically disappeared. It felt great.

"Thanks, dude. I don't know what you did, but you can do it anytime."

"You're welcome. Where are we off to now?" Johnny settled in, seatbelt tightly in place.

"Well, I don't know where you're going. Off to a cloud to catch some shuteye, maybe? But me, I'm going to check on a little boy." Liam headed in the direction where the Ruiz family lived. He turned on the

radio and let the music soothe. As he pulled up to a corner, he looked in a grocery store's large window and, with the sun at the perfect angle, saw his car and himself, but the passenger seat was unsurprisingly empty. Gave him goose bumps, since the pirate sprawled in full sight.

Once he arrived, he slowed down perceptibly, having learned his lesson. The street was clear, and there was a place to park in front of the house with the rundown façade. Since he'd put up the convertible top, he stooped to get out of the car and hesitated, then turned in the direction of the fellow who rested in the passenger seat. Liam's one arm held open the door while the other leaned against the frame. *"You coming?"*

"For the time being, I'm comfy here. Don't hurry."

"You're going to trust me alone?"

"You'll do splendidly, I have no doubt."

Liam slammed the door and walked away muttering. "Sure! I can't get rid of him when he isn't wanted, and now when I could use some backup, he's too comfy to move. Bast...!" He cut himself off before finishing the word. "Guess I can't even call him names."

As he approached the stairs, he heard crying, and the sound of it made him take the steps two at a time. He knocked and then noticed the door hadn't been closed all the way. He stepped into the room.

Pedro, the child, was sobbing heartbrokenly as

he knelt beside his mother, who lay on the floor in a pool of water. Liam ran towards them to check the woman and soothe the boy. "What happened, Pedro?" His rough voice seemed to shock the boy out of his hysterics, and with a glad cry he flung himself at Liam. "*Mi mamá* is dying. Help her, *señor*, please."

A soft pleading came from the pregnant woman who had arched her body, contorting it this way and that. "Sir, the baby is coming. You must call my midwife."

The pain seemed to intensify, as if it intended to break up her insides. She writhed in agony, biting her lips bloody to stop the screams. Once the contraction had passed, she whispered to Liam, "Take him away from this. He mustn't see."

"What is going on here?" A very angry dude, dressed in working-man's clothes and big boots, stood in the doorway rooted to the spot. "Isobella!" Once he'd taken in the details, he dropped his lunchbox and rushed to kneel next to Liam. "*Papá*," Pedro reached for his father, leaving Liam's arms without a moment's hesitation. "Help *mamá*. She's sick."

"I'm calling an ambulance." Liam whipped out his cell phone and would have dialed 911 if the other fellow hadn't ripped it from his hands and flung it across the room.

"No ambulance. Her midwife. I'll call." Settling the boy on his hip, he rose then rushed to the telephone table by the wall, where a small book lay open.

Liam watched as he dialed the number, and when he felt a trembling hand clutch his, he encircled her fingers reassuringly. "Don't worry, honey. We'll get you some help." A glance told him the woman worked miracles to keep the shrieks from breaking loose. Her lips were torn and raw while tears poured from her eyes nonstop. First he patted her shoulder. Then he cleared the damp mass of wild curls away from her face.

Behind him, Liam heard the Spanish torrent of pleas, and because he was multi-lingual in four different languages, Spanish being his best, he knew immediately from the one-sided conversation that the midwife couldn't be reached. *Son of a bitch!* He had no idea how to birth a baby, and he wasn't sure her husband did, either. He'd seen the look of horror and fear on the other man's face.

"Look Mr. Ruiz, this is an emergency. Your wife needs a doctor, and I have no idea of how to help her. Do you?"

"Yes. I can look after her if you'll help. There's no time to argue. The baby will come quickly if she has the same delivery as she did with Pedro. Go to the kitchen, boil the kettle, and take the boy with you." Saying this, he forcefully held out the boy, who'd been twisted around him like ivy growing on the north side of a building. "Bring the clean towels from the drawer. Pedro, you show the hombre where *mamá* keeps them." Ruiz ran to kneel beside his woman and began to position pillows under her back from the nearby sofa.

Shocked to his core, Liam felt as if a brick had been slammed into his face. This guy couldn't be serious. "Hey, bud. She needs a doctor."

"No, she needs help. Now go!" Ruiz pointed to a doorway, then began loosening her clothing and removing her pants. When he realized that Liam stood glued to the spot, he yelled again, louder and made a move, as if to threaten. "Go!" This time the man bellowed and Liam felt an unknown force push him forward.

Liam went.

Being separated from both his parents, the boy screamed with ferocity, the decibels rising. Oh god, where the hell was the angel when he needed him? He'd rather face a battalion of rioting enemy soldiers than deal with a hysterical brat.

"Shush, big guy. We need to help your mom now, okay?" Once in the kitchen, he lowered the boy and knelt in front of him. The wet cheeks and big terrified eyes got to him, and he swiped gently at the tears and gave a quick reassuring hug. "Your dad gave us a job to do, so we need to follow orders. You go get me the towels your papa wants, and I'll fill the kettle."

Giving the boy a little push to start him off, he quickly ran to the stove, turned it on high, and grabbed the kettle. He let the hot water run until it steamed, filled the thing, and placed it on the red burner.

Spying the washroom, he flew in and checked out the medicine cabinet. Happier than a pig in shit, he found what he wanted, a big bottle of hydrogen peroxide. It stopped infection. He knew it worked. During his childhood, when he'd collected the cuts and scrapes of an active child, his father had used this as an effective treatment.

His dad! Funny how the thought popped into his head just then, as if he needed to think of things like that now. But the truth was it had always been his father who'd kept his head in moments of stress. Unlike his mother, who'd normally screech for her husband.

"*Señor*. Here are the towels." The little guy held so many in his chubby arms that they trailed on the floor behind him and the weight almost toppled him over.

"Good boy." Liam lifted them from him. "Now you go in the kitchen, watch the kettle, and yell when it's boiling, okay? And don't touch anything." Liam remembered to add that last bit. Who knew what went through a child's mind when he wanted to help.

Pedro nodded and ran over to stand guard in front of the stove.

Liam hightailed it back into the living room and saw that Ruiz had gotten his wife undressed and covered with a blanket. He was crouched down between her knees.

As soon as he heard Liam, he looked up, his expression calm while his eyes screamed *"Help!"*

"I found the disinfectant; you should clean your hands." Liam flung the towels down next the man and steered clear of the working area.

"Where is Pedro?"

"I have him watching the kettle; he'll call when it's boiling."

Grunts and whimpers broke loose as Isobela's body reacted to another contraction. Liam could feel the pain rippling through his own in sympathy. He tightened his muscles and his butt cheeks clenched.

The wild-eyed glance from Ruiz scared the daylights out of him. "You know what to do, right?"

"Yeah! Yeah! I need scissors. We need them to cut the cord. They should be in the kitchen drawer. And a big pot, from the cupboard under the sink."

Isobela's cracked lips opened, and her tired voice stuttered. "The suitcase—baby clothes—hallway."

"*Papá,* the water is ready." Pedro rocked back and forth in the doorway, his legs scissored.

"Good, *mi hijo.* Now go to the toilet like a big boy." His telling glance at Liam pleaded.

"Come, Pedro, I'll help you. You have to show me where your mom keeps her scissors. He took the boy's extended hand and led him to the bathroom, where the boy fetched a stepping platform, stood on it, and pulled down his pants.

"You okay, big guy?" Liam waited for Pedro's nod, fondled his hair, and then backed away. I need to get the water." He rushed to the kitchen and fetched the big pot, pouring it half full of boiling water. Finding the scissors, he threw them into the water to soak and hefted the pot with the handle to carry to where Isobel's nightmare progressed. In the hallway, her suitcase leaned against the wall, and he grabbed that also.

"I'm boiling the scissors, but they'll still need to be washed with the peroxide."

"Good idea. The baby's coming, I can see the head. Help Isobela. She needs to lean against you now."

"Who, me?"

"Do it!"

Liam settled behind the exhausted woman and lifted her shoulders gently so they rested back against his chest. He grabbed a towel, leaned over her to wipe the sweat from her face, and asked soothingly. "Comfy?"

"Yes-s, *gracias*." She let her body weight fall back trustingly.

Liam noticed the painfully dry edges on each side of her mouth. He scanned the room and sure enough, there was Pedro crouched under a wooden chair, watching. "Hey, kiddo, can you get your mom some ice from the freezer?"

The boy nodded and jumped up to disappear.

And at that moment, Liam watched as Isobela's stomach rippled and her legs splayed. After a moment, she balanced her heels on the floor, reached for his hand, and using it as a counterweight, the little warrior began to push. He felt as if she'd be ripping his arms from their sockets before she stopped. And no sooner did he get to rest for a moment but she started again, this time almost in a sitting position.

"*Perfecto, mi amor.*" Ruiz's face, sweaty as his wife's, beamed for a moment from above the blanket. Then his head disappeared once again. His voice came muffled but understandable "The baby comes soon. Push once more."

"Ahhhh!!" The scream tore from her before she scrunched her face for the final grunting thrust.

Liam heard Ruiz's gasp of joy and felt intoxicated himself from the swell of relief. The baby's cry sounded loud and annoyed.

"*Una bebé niña! Una niña Hermosa!* Beautiful! She's beautiful." The proud father cried the words, taking sobbing breaths between each phrase, tears cascading down unshaven cheeks. He wrapped a towel around the infant and laid her over his lap.

Isobela fell back against Liam and sighed deeply, her hand wiping her face before reaching for the babe. "*Darla a mi.*"

Liam felt his own body sobbing inside and tried desperately to stop the tears that wanted to fall.

He shared a moment with the proud mother that would be etched forever in his memory, and then propped her with the pillows. On his knees he crawled to where Ruiz had collapsed, seemingly useless now that the worst of the trauma had passed. Not thinking, he reached in the water for the scissors.

"Son of a bit... god, that's hot!" Just in time he spied the boy crawling to his mother, holding out a prized piece of ice. He hefted the pot in his hands and returned to the kitchen to pour out the water so they could retrieve the tool they needed. And then he hurried back to Ruiz, who waited with the hydrogen peroxide. Once they'd soaked the scissors long enough to be sure, the two looked at each other and hesitated.

Liam spoke first. "I'll hold it and you cut."

"We need string. We need to tie it." The man looked around as if he'd never seen the house before.

It was Isobela who chimed in and made sense. "The telephone table." She pointed, and Liam cautiously handed the slimy grayish umbilical cord back to Ruiz. He'd disarm a live bomb any day over this ordeal. He scuttled to the table and back, string clutched in his sore hands. In moments the deed was done and the noisy infant lay cuddled in her mother's arms.

"Chico," said Ruiz, dragging his son's rapt attention from his new baby sister. "Go and get two beers from the fridge for me and *mi amigo, por favor*."

His raised eyebrow asked and Liam's nod answered. The two men, shoulders slumped, drew deep breaths while their eyes stayed glued to the charming performance of a mother meeting her daughter for the first time.

Just then, the outside door was flung open and a middle-aged woman dashed into the house, only to stop dead at the sight of her patient holding the newborn. At a glance, she seemed to know what to do and quickly took control, pushing her way between the men and taking charge. With a very few terse questions, she deemed everything to be in order.

Liam backed away and watched as Ruiz scooped wife and baby into his arms. He hugged them so tenderly that Liam once again had to bite down hard.

Since both he and the boy were superfluous, Liam led him into the kitchen, to the table, and sat him on top. After he shut the open freezer door, he looked to see if there was anything in the fridge for the boy to drink while he sucked up his beer in three swallows. "Want some Coke?" He'd seen a can on the door.

"*Mi mamá* says no pop—only milk and juice." Pedro caught his eye and leaned toward him. "I have a new sister?"

"Yes, and she's beautiful." He took the apple

juice carton and snagged a glass to fill halfway. Once the boy held it, Liam clinked his bottle against it in a toast and said, "Here's to the new princess Ruiz."

Obviously loving the attention, Pedro giggled. "She's all red."

"Uh-huh!"

"And wrinkly."

"Yep."

"And she screams really loud."

"Oh, yeah!"

"Do we have to keep her?"

Maybe he shouldn't have laughed, but nothing in the world could have stopped the waves from bursting loose. He picked the boy up in his arms, and all the while he hugged, he swung him around in a circle, loving the happy squeals. "She'll be your best friend one day, little guy. You'd better take care of her."

"Okay, okay-y!"

The door opened and Ruiz slowly stepped into the room, his shoulders slumped like those of a beaten man. It reminded Liam a little of someone else he'd seen recently.

Ruiz plucked his son from Liam's arms, hugged him for a second, and then lowered him. "*Tu mamá* wants you, *mi hijo*."

Once the door closed and the two men had nowhere else to look, Ruiz turned to Liam and held out his hand. Liam slapped it away and shoved his face right up close to the other man.

Chapter 10

"What the hell is wrong with you? What if something had happened, if the baby hadn't come properly or... or something? She could have died in the hands of two bloody incompetent idiots who had no reason to take chances with her life. You're a fool! Why the hell wouldn't you let me call the ambulance?" Liam lowered his voice for the last part when he'd noticed Ruiz's warning glance aimed toward the other room.

"Easy for you to say, *Señor*. I no have health insurance. I am here illegally. What do you know? You think the doctors would have treated her?" Veins stood out on his forehead, and his bloodshot eyes pierced Liam's conscience. "Why do you think we hired a midwife?"

With both hands held in front, Liam took a step back and calmed down. "Look, I'm sorry. I didn't know. I would have paid for her treatment in a second."

"But I have no money to pay you back. I work long hard hours and get paid *nada*." Ruiz's fingers rubbed together, his expression disgusted. "Gringos like to take advantage of a man who can't fight back."

"Not all gringos. What kind of work do you do?"

"Anything! Dig ditches, clean sewers, work in a kitchen, whatever I can find. But the pay is bad, if I even get paid. My big-shot boss stiffed me today and... Look, I'm not complaining. We're here in America, safe from the drug cartel on the streets of Ciudad Juarez. So no matter what happens, we are better off."

"You're mixed up in the drug trade back home." Liam couldn't help the disgust evident in his words.

"No! Never! They forced Isobela's father to work for them, and then they killed him. The *escoria*... how you say...?"

"... scum."

"*Si!* They think Isobela witnessed this-this *atrocidad*—"

"Atrocity?"

"*Si!* And they want to kill her so she can't testify. But she saw nothing. We fled with only the clothes we wore."

Liam could see the man was done. He looked so tired that he reminded him of soldiers coming off days of advanced training, exhausted and beaten.

"I'll leave you to your family now, but I'd like to come back and talk to you again, if I may? I might have a job for you, one that will pay proper wages for the hours you work."

Hope lit the man's eyes. A little light that started small, then flared and grew as he stared at Liam and looked into his soul.

"You are the man in this morning's accident, *si?*"

"*Si!*"

"Then I owe you twice. You have managed to save both my children today."

"No. You have it wrong. You saved your daughter, and Miss Bertolli saved your son. Twice I've managed to be in the wrong place at the wrong time."

Chapter 11

By early Sunday, Sadie's patience with the family scene had vanished. She had to get out of the loony bin. Of course, before her wacky mother would let her leave, she'd called Greta to be sure she'd be home. In case Sadie got into trouble. What the heck kind of trouble did she think Sadie might get into?

Thank heavens Greta had answered and agreed to stick around. Yet they still balked. Finally, she sweet-talked them with promises. Like spending the next weekend together at their beach house for a pajama party. They'd watch chick flicks and eat junk food. It didn't seem too dreadful to her right now, but she knew when the time came that would change. It was their idea of a good time. And her idea of a nightmare.

But right now, she'd do anything to get away

from their constant singing, their mind-numbing cheeriness, and their maddening references to her new boyfriend, spoken with tongue in cheek, of course. Any chance to tease, they took.

Right from the beginning, their sickeningly sweet tones had warned her of just how much they'd taken to Liam. If that wasn't enough, the proof became very clear in the way they'd opened up to him while he'd been their guest. They'd talked to him about business, things that would normally only be shared between the family. They'd lit up when he praised their food. In fact, you'd think the player had never had a well-cooked meal before he met "the sweet gals," as he'd referred to them more than once. All the time he overstayed his welcome—in her opinion—he'd overplayed his part and they'd simpered disgustingly.

Considering that they had very few men to cater to, since neither of her sisters had a serious beau at the time, nor her mom, she supposed she shouldn't mind so much that they'd sucked up to Liam like glaze on a honey donut.

But she did.

Both her sisters had made a play for his attention. When that didn't seem to work, since he teased them equally, they did their best to sing her praises.

It had curdled her stomach.

Chapter 12

Early Monday afternoon, at the approximate time specified and the address Bea had written down, Liam showed up ready and willing for work—more fool he!

Impatient, Sadie stood clicking her booted heel against the sidewalk—fists planted on her hips. Her tight sweater and jean-clad body drew stares from other drivers, but she never even noticed. She was too busy eyeballing her watch, and as he approached, her eyes drilled him.

The words popped out before he could stop them. "Traffic was slow."

"Not the way you drive."

"I had an unwanted guest who kept me within the speed limit."

He watched her look at his car, angle her head questioningly and then turn back his way.

"He got out on the last block. You're obviously ready so let's go."

"Not in this pretty toy you call a car. We'll have to use the company vehicle." He should have known something was up when her checks reddened.

Hobbling along by his side, she led him into the underground parking lot right up to the ugliest monstrosity on four wheels he'd ever seen—a rosy pink doggie van with splashes of paw prints streaked to run along each side. The hideous, doggy, shag-mobile was outfitted with a penned-in back where the animals rode, each with their own windows and special enclosures reminiscent of baby seats.

She frowned at him when he couldn't stifle his horror. "Don't you say a word! My mother and sisters bought this through the company when they realized my own car was too small to transport the animals safely. They ordered it specially designed and painted, and if you'd been there to see their expressions when they presented it to me, you couldn't have refused their generosity either."

He grinned.

She glared.

Then he helped her step up into the passenger seat, got behind the wheel, and drove it out onto the street. The silence had thickened, so he spoke.

"No, really! It's roomy. And the pink is... is eye-catching. Paw designs, are a good way to advertise."

She said nothing, but she did snort.

"We're getting lots of attention." *Yeah, everyone's laughing!* Words popped into his head coming straight from his conscience.

He hated himself for lying, and the truth must have showed in his sour expression.

"Not funny! And slow it down, especially when the dogs are with us. They'll get antsy if you go too fast."

"And you know that how?"

"Never mind... and lose the grin." Even though her voice sounded rough, the chuckle he heard negated her being in a real snit.

"Yes, ma'am." Maybe the stares won't be so hard to take after all. It was nice being with Sadie again. She looked stunning with her soft curls bouncing around her pretty face. He'd looked forward to spending the afternoon with her, and if it meant driving a pink puppy parlor, he guessed he could take it.

After all, guys who had a firm grip on their sexuality didn't get rattled with minor shit like this. And if the asshole in the car next to his didn't stop wiggling his eyebrows and smirking, he'd be more than happy to rearrange his face at the next light.

"Liam. Quit glowering at everyone and listen. Please. I have to explain a few facts before we start the day. I don't want you to undo all the work it's taken me months to put into practice. My students are in training, and unless you do exactly as I tell you, it won't be pretty."

"Students? I thought they were dogs."

"They are dogs, silly. But they're my students, also. I train them during these walking exercises, and they respond very well—to me. I just don't know whether you'll be smart enough."

"Now you're just being mean and... and rude."

"I'm not being rude. These dogs are very intelligent. They know whenever they can get away with anything, and like children they'll try to take over, be the pack leader. It's up to you to stay in control—to show them who's boss."

"Lady, if I can get through Special Forces training and work with some of the young idiots people are producing today, I have no doubt I can handle a few mutts."

"Don't be too hasty. Or ignore my advice."

"I'm sure I'll be just fine." He gave her his best don't-worry-about-me-little-lady nod, and she closed her mouth and crossed her arms.

Eating his own words didn't come easy to him. Begging didn't either, but by the time he'd walked the first pack for one block, had been tripped and almost upended, had the chains wrapped around his legs so he'd had to sit down on the sidewalk in order to get loose, and stopped a dozen times to undo leashes and rearrange their order, he'd begun to worry. The final straw came during one of the leash removals when the smallest in the group,

Peppi the Pomeranian, had taken the opportunity to break loose. After he'd chased him three blocks before catching the poufy-haired little bugger, he knew he needed to listen.

The fact that Johnny-come-lately witnessed his disgrace didn't help either. By the time Liam got back to where Sadie had the dogs properly behaving as they all waited for his return, he was hot under the collar and felt pretty damn foolish.

To see the devil glinting from the angel's eyes didn't help the situation whatsoever. *"Why don't you go hug a cloud?"*

"And miss all the fun? Not likely!"

"Liam, are you now ready to take some advice?"

"I'm all ears!" Go figure. Six dogs could be so hard to handle? He looked at the well-behaved monsters now arranged around Sadie, who sat like a queen on the park bench with her roll of plastic doggie bags on her lap, and he motioned his surrender.

"Okay, first you'll have to pick up the poop that Nicky and Reverend left just over by the trees. Here's the bags." She unrolled two smallish bags and held them out.

He wasn't sure if he'd heard her properly. Did she just ask him to pick up dog shit in a baggy?

"Cor. The stuff won't bite you. Blokes pick up dog droppings all the time."

"Not this bloke."

"So you're going to make Sadie do it when she

can barely walk, never mind bend over?"

Liam stomped over to her and whipped the bags from her hands. "Where are they?"

She pointed. He purposely didn't look her in the eye, because if she was enjoying this moment, which he had no doubt she was, being a nice guy, he didn't want to spoil it for her. Plus, he knew the squeamishness he felt in his gut had to be splashed across his mug. He wasn't enough of an actor to hide it.

A damn good thing the litter can stood only a few feet away.

Holding the bags out at arm's length would have drawn a bit more attention than he wanted if he'd had to go any farther.

"*Give over, ya toff. Don't be daft. It's a natural function.*"

"*Be quiet! I did it, didn't I? When I was a kid I wasn't allowed to have a dog. So this is all new to me.*"

The angel's attitude instantly underwent a change. "*I know, Liam. You did good, my man.*" So saying, Johnny disappeared and left a rush of gladness behind that dissolved all the anxiety insideLiam. Left him feeling strangely happy.

He went back to Sadie. She was speaking softly to the dogs, which were rapt with attention, all six pairs of eyes glazed with adoration. In his mind, they were walking a strange assortment of mutts. And he guessed he shouldn't think of these expensive, groomed-to-their-eyeballs, manicured babies as mutts, but in his mind that's exactly what they were.

Stunned at how people could spend the amount of money it took to not only buy the animals but maintain their perfect styling, he studied each one.

Peppi, his personal favorite, the mutt who'd shown gumption by getting away when he had the chance, was a reddish-gold ball of fluff whose little black, beady eyes seemed to see everything. At the same time his tongue lolled to the side and his open mouth curved upwards in a distinctly cheeky way.

Lying next to him was a gorgeous white Samoyed called Samantha who had a similar laughing expression and a large plumed tail that never stopped waving.

Then came Giorgio, a standard white Poodle, who had to be dragged along, as walking didn't appeal to him much. According to Sadie, he'd won Best of Breed in many shows and was the particularly spoiled baby of a wealthy heiress.

Next to him a German Shepherd called Nicky displayed leadership qualities by marshalling the others back into position with a nip or a bark, then looked angelic when Sadie called him on his tactics. He was a strong son-of-a-gun who'd almost torn Liam's arm from the socket during a few tussles.

Lying next to him, totally bored and showing it, was the ugliest of the happy little group, Reverend, a wrinkled mass of fawn-colored skin whose eyes disappeared periodically. According to Sadie, Shar-Pei dogs were a relatively new breed, intelligent and loving. Maybe so, but dragging one along in a group of six wasn't easy.

Just then the yappy one started up again. A miniature Pinscher, or Min-Pin as she called it, took the prize for its annoying habit of never shutting up. Liam visualized wrapping his hands around the small neck and squeez—

"Liam? Where did you go? I've called you twice. We have another group to walk in a short while, so we need to get moving."

"Right, sorry. Was thinking about how different these breeds are and how each one of these mutts perform."

"They're very smart, you know."

"I have no problem with real dogs, ones that have faces and paws, not these powder puffs with feet." First he pointed at the Giorgio and then Peppi.

"Are you dissing my pack?" Her smiling eyes downplayed the harshness in her tone.

"I just can't imagine how any normal person would put so much importance into a four-legged barker—seems to me that people should come first." Once the words hung out there, he realized he sounded pretty insensitive and felt the disintegration start in his backbone and work its way down to his weakening knees. What an idiot, running off at the mouth like that.

With a warning glint in her eye, Sadie spoke softly. "You must admit, when I have control, they're very well behaved. Some are show dogs, after all, and worth a small fortune."

He scanned the wagging, squirmy bunch. What he figured was the money spent on a poodle with a glittery necklace of pink gems gracing her neck and a rhinestone-studded harness around her body could feed a village in some of the countries where he'd travelled.

As if he sensed his importance, Giorgio pranced forward, his backcombed pompoms waving in circles and his tiny black eyes blinking in a flirtatious manner.

Liam backed away. The doggy grin allowed a glimpse of sharp teeth, and the low growl portrayed a problematic attitude.

Just then the German shepherd, Nicky, stepped between them, using his body as a shield. He nipped at the poodle, which sniffed and turned away. "Now there's a dog a man can be proud to walk."

Liam reached to pat the regal head and just managed to retrieve all his digits before they were snapped off by the sharp jaws.

"What the hell...?"

Sadie's grin showed off her pearly whites. "First of all, Nicky has an attitude problem, and secondly, you never wave your hand toward an animal unless he knows you and is relaxed around you. They don't like it. It intimidates them."

"No kidding! So what's Nicky's beef with the world?"

"He doesn't like men, but he's got a heart the size of Mount Rushmore."

"And the teeth of a crocodile."

"At least he's honest in his reactions, and let's the world see who he is, unlike some people I know." She stared at him with purposeful directness.

He shuffled and turned away to hide his dismay. She'd gotten to know him pretty well in a very short time. He needed to change the subject.

"You mentioned that you teach these dogs tricks?"

"I don't teach them tricks. I train them."

"Train them, you mean like—how to shake a paw and roll over?"

"Those easy parlor tricks they learned in no time at all. Most of these dogs are incredibly clever and aren't satisfied with the easy stuff. Now we work on harder trials like fetch and count and..."

"Count? How can a dog count?"

"Watch."

"Gorgio..." She waited until the poodle deigned to lift his head and look her way. "How many fingers?" She held up three and the fluff ball barked three times. Then she asked, "Are you sure?" And the dog nodded. "How many now?" She lowered one of the fingers and the dog barked twice. "See?"

"Pretty good! What other tricks did you teach it?"

"It's not an it. It's a he."

"That's a male?" Liam glared at the animal and said, "You oughta be ashamed." The fluffy canine looked down at the ground and a small whine could be heard as he turned away.

Sadie shared the humorous moment with him before going on with her explanation.

"I train the dogs because if they aren't properly schooled, I can't accept them into the walking program. Also, bored dogs are sad, and my friends are never sad. Many of these guys have been used in movies." The pride rang through her tone. "Don't let their appearance belie their intelligence."

"In other words, you *can* teach an old dog new tricks." He grinned at his silly pun.

"Canine ones. Humans, not so easy. Especially the male of the species." Her eyes held a definite twinkle.

"You're not funny!"

Chapter 13

After she and Liam had finished with the first round of walkers, they followed up with three more groups till the light waned in the sky and darkness was still just a warning. Sadie had talked Liam through the afternoon's route and she felt surprisingly pleased with the results. Once she'd instilled the importance of how to hold the leashes, tone of voice, and the physical strength that kept them moving and stopped any shenanigans, everything worked out very well.

"I know you do this every day, and I'm truly amazed. Anyone who believes dog-walkers have it easy needs to give their head a shake." The sincerity she heard in his voice began to unwind the tight ball she constantly carried around in her stomach whenever she spent time with a man.

Her sisters and mother had tried to talk to her

about carrying her teenage hostilities into her life as an adult. But when a vulnerable young girl gets a certain kind of unwanted attention from idiot teenage males, the kind that rips out hearts and makes a girl cry herself to sleep every night, it's damned hard to let go of the deep bitterness.

For some, like her sisters, being overweight never created a problem. They sailed through their school years with a huge group of friends and were very popular. But Sadie was different.

Introverted, shy, a slim girl imprisoned in a large body with no way out and no one to turn to, she'd struggled year after year. When she did try to explain her feelings to her family, they took it personally, and she could see that if she continued down that road their feelings would take a beating. Of course, that wasn't an option. And so she ate their food, laughed at their foolish ways, and bided her time until she couldn't take it anymore.

Then, like a miracle, Greta came along to save her sanity. Her roommate in college let Sadie be herself, and she blossomed. She took many courses on good dietary habits, and even cooking classes, and put them all to good use.

Just before they graduated, Greta's aunt had built the condo complex and was looking for residents she trusted to take care of the property. Greta grabbed the first suite and put in a good word for Sadie. Since then, life had been great. Other than the pressure her family applied for her to find a boyfriend, happiness had finally found her. She had a job she loved and a peaceful place of her own to unwind, so what more could she ask?

The little bites her emotions suffered periodically when she watched a romantic movie or a love story on television was a small price to pay when it came to protecting her heart.

Battered by memories still vivid enough to awaken her at night, she rued the day she'd let a high-school stud sweet-talk her guard down long enough for him to get into her pants and then post it on Facebook.

Never again—no way, no how.

So when Liam asked to come in for a while after they finished work, her response came easy.

"Why?"

"Ahh, because?"

"Not good enough."

"I thought we could have a beer and discuss the day. You could fill me in on the dogs, like their backgrounds, especially your favorites."

The sweet-talker knew where to stroke. But it wouldn't do him any good. Not with her.

Before she could send him on his way, Greta pulled her Jeep up beside them and started a conversation.

"Hey, girlfriend! How was your day?" All the time she talked, she batted her eyes at Liam and smiled in the toothy way that she used on anyone with a penis and lips.

Sadie sighed and surveyed the underground garage's white ceilings, pipes, and the horizontal florescent fixtures. A nudge from Liam got her attention, and she saw the other two waited for her to make introductions.

"My friend, Greta." She waved at the simpering idiot whose head was sticking out the window, and then pointed at the guy beside her. "Speedy Gonzales, who prefers you call him Liam."

"Hey, Liam. I've heard all about you." After the hissing sound and glower that came from Sadie, she added, "From Bea, Sadie's mom. She said you'd be helping her *sweet little girl* with the dogs for the next while. Lucky bitches!"

Only Greta could get away with sarcastic teasing that would break Sadie's restraint and make her laugh.

"Hey, you two, here's the thing. I've got the makings for the biggest stir-fry you've ever seen, and I'm expecting my last-night's date in about half an hour. Why don't you join us?"

"We'd love to."

"Not a chance."

When Liam turned to Sadie, obviously to see just how serious her refusal, she knew he made note that her eyes were still lit with humor. She couldn't help it. Greta could always make her laugh.

She sensed him trying to think of the right words to convince her to change her mind, but

Greta took the situation into her own hands.

"Give me twenty minutes to change, and then be prepared to be put to work as my underpaid whipping boys." So saying, she peeled away to park further down the garage.

Sadie stamped her foot and the painful reminder from her sore body made her catch her breath. Maybe she'd overdone it a tad. Should have sat and let him walk the dogs alone, but she'd been a bit leery. Good thing, too, since he'd had some close calls at getting his legs broken and his hands ripped off.

"Are you happy?" Her growl seemed to delight him. "Why did you encourage her? Now we'll have to go, or she'll be after me, and I couldn't handle it right now."

"You sure do hate having people mad at you, don't you, darling?"

"Not you. So don't get any ideas. Give me a hand. I'm more tired than I thought. I'd better get a couple of pills in me if I mean to last the rest of the evening. Just so you know. We eat and then we leave."

"Got it! Eat, leave. Do you think this could be counted as our first date?"

"I'm not going to credit that absurd comment with a response. Stop that cackling!" She hid her smile by putting her arm through his and leaned heavily. If she could get to her medicine cabinet and the bottle of Tylenol her mother had insisted she take home, for once in her life, she'd give over and listen to orders.

***

Greta's new friend, Stan, turned out to be a complete surprise. Sandy-colored hair, a slim build, and a nice smile all worked in his favor to make Sadie decide to like him. That and the fact that he also had a wicked sense of fun, which kept everyone laughing at his sharp comebacks while Greta and Liam egged him on.

Greta, who'd calmed down her usual stick-out-everywhere hairstyle to a softer, more appealing look, glowed as the evening passed. She'd chosen her outfit to be less revealing than usual, and her flowing slacks and filmy blouse gave her a more demure appearance. Sadie approved the look and hugged her friend when they were cleaning up the mess in the kitchen.

"I like your Stan. He's a lot of fun and seems really nice. And he hasn't taken his eyes off you all evening."

"Funny. I was going to say the same thing to you about Liam. He's studly." She kissed the air and then planted one on Sadie's cheek. "He's also really nice and smart and tall and clean and smells good and—"

"All right already. I get it. You like him." Sadie scowled, gulped, and then added, "Fine! So do I. But he's not for me. A guy like him needs a fancy lady, not an ordinary girl." Before Greta could argue, Sadie continued, "Hon, I'm sore all over. I have to go and lie down before I fall down."

She limped to the door, waved, and then walked into the living room to overhear the guys still laughing and joking.

"I'm off now. I need to get a hot bath. See you tomorrow, Liam, earlier time, same place. Nice meeting you, Stan." Before she could even open the door, Liam, moving more quickly than a big man should be able to, gently pushed her aside.

"I'll take you over."

"I do know the way home. Stay and visit."

"Hey, when I take a girl out, I bring her home." He waved to the other two, who had followed them to the door, complimented the chef, shook hands with Stan, and then twisted the knob, which he'd covered with his big hand so she couldn't just leave.

As soon as they entered her kitchen, she headed through the low-lit condo to the front door, where she knew his car was still parked along the front curb. And being a fast learner, before he could grab the knob as he had earlier, she palmed it and pulled the door open. He needed to leave. Little nerves were having a field day in her tummy, and she worried that her voice would tremble and give her away. "Don't be late tomorrow." There. She'd carried that off well.

He caught her eye and mesmerized her by the intent look in his. Sultry, compelling, actually wicked, his stare wouldn't let up, and her fear grew to where she felt like she'd choke. All she could do was watch to see what would happen next. That's without letting herself pant like a dog in heat.

He leaned in and put both hands on either side of her face. Holding her prisoner, he moved nearer and whispered, "Sleep well. I'll see you just after lunch." Then he rubbed his nose gently against hers, and she could swear she heard him moan. Once the heat in his gaze warned of his arousal, confirming he was physically affected, he lowered his surprisingly lush lashes and turned away. With his back facing her, he stopped and said in a voice unlike his own, "Till tomorrow."

Chapter 14

The next morning, after Isobela peeked out the window and saw Liam standing on the doorstep with a big pink teddy under one arm and a brown one under the other, she flung the door wide and beckoned him to enter. He also clutched a bouquet of flowers in one hand, and a box of chocolates in the other and wondered if he looked as foolish as he felt.

Glad when she closed the door to shut out any interested observers, he took a moment to study the tear tracks on her face. She'd been crying. His heart leaped into his throat.

Situations that spoke of disharmony made him feel squeamish, and most of the time, he'd get away at the first opportunity. Possibly it reminded him too much of his childhood, a time in his life he rarely let himself return to, because whenever he did, he was screwed up for days.

"*Señor* Liam! I'm glad to see you. Are these for me?" Isobela motioned to the flowers he held awkwardly.

"Ahhh, yes! Yes, the flowers are for you, and the chocolates—"

"*Señor* Liam!" Little feet running as fast as they could, Pedro flung himself towards the tall man without a worry as to whether he'd be caught. Dropping the teddies, Liam bent just in time for the boy to wrap his arms around his neck. As he lifted him, he got an extra hard hug. The affection that glowed on the chubby features gave him such a thrill that an empty space in his chest filled and began to expand. *Wow!*

Looking at the two happy faces that smiled back, shyness attacked and he stammered. "I brought teddy bears for the kids. I didn't know what else..." Just then Ruiz appeared, standing tall and looking angry.

"*Buenos días*, Liam. You brought my family presents. How nice!"

His tone and the words didn't jibe. Liam felt Pedro's body stiffen. The hairs on the back of Liam's neck stood waving for attention. If they could speak, they'd be saying, "Oh-oh"!

"Hey, Ruiz. Just wanted to stop by and see if everything was fine with the baby. Had to bring some gifts 'cause that's what people do when they come visiting, right?"

Liam hoped by reminding Ruiz of the social niceties, he'd cut him some slack. He didn't know what was stuck in the other man's craw, but he bloody well didn't intend to take any guff, either.

Isobela, who held the chocolates and flowers as if they were precious, spoke softly, a warning tone in evidence, and her husband responded immediately.

"*Mi amor*. Liam came to pay his respects and is our guest. I will go and put on the coffee. Pedro, thank Liam for your teddy bear, and then put the one for Teresa by her crib."

"*Si, mamá. Gracias, Señor* Liam. I like brown bears the best." Pedro sneered at the pink bear tellingly.

Grinning, Liam lowered him and watched as the small boy struggled to carry the two large, fluffy, bow-tied bears.

"Come, Liam, in the kitchen so we can talk. The baby sleeps here in the living room, and she just now stopped crying."

"Is everything okay?"

"Babies cry." Isobela shrugged. As she slowly began to lead the way into the other room, Liam saw the worry she couldn't hide. She took small steps while holding her side. Again, niggling feelings made his stomach tighten. "Come, Angelo. We will have coffee." She pushed gently at her husband's arm to steer him in front of her.

Liam sat across the scuffed wooden table from Ruiz, who he couldn't think of in any other way.

He guessed he'd have to start using his real name, but somehow Angelo didn't seem to suit the man. Without thinking, he asked the first question that came to mind, and then wished he could rip out his tongue when he saw the other's expression.

"How come you're not at work?"

"You come to visit my wife when I'm away?" Angelo spit the sentence out. Anger raged inside that he couldn't hide.

"I didn't intend to come in, just wanted to know that the baby was healthy." Liam knew he could be intimidating. Behind his back, his men made jokes about him being a hard-assed prick. To his face, they nicknamed him Iceman. Since this guy needed to learn a few lessons on manners, he purposely gave him the look that he knew worked. And it did this time also.

Angelo deflated. "*Si!* It was very kind of you. I'm being a jerk. I apologize."

Isobela hovered in the background, and Liam could feel her anxiety. And when Pedro crept into the room, he went to lean against his mother's knee and wrapped his arms around her as if he needed her strength. *What the hell is going on here?*

Bluntly, Liam asked the question that hung in the air for seconds and made the uncomfortable atmosphere worse. "What happened?"

The silence continued as he looked first at Angelo and then at Isobela. It was Pedro who spoke. "My papa got fired. The bad man phoned him not to come to work and won't pay him his money."

Obviously little pitchers did have big ears, as the saying goes, because Pedro had heard everything.

Liam looked over at the other man, who stared fixedly at the table and rubbed at the worn spot.

"Screw him. I've got work for you anytime you're ready. Hard work, but then, you said you didn't mind how hard you had to work. That's right, isn't it?"

The hope that filled the other man's face made Liam glad he'd spoken before he'd thought of the consequences. The consequences being that he'd now be forced to visit his dad. He'd seen the old man struggling to rake the leaves. He'd also seen the disrepair that his childhood house was in and knew it needed a lot of care. Obviously, his father tried to do all the work himself, but he was getting on, and the property was huge.

Before he could take back his words, he added, "After coffee I'll take you over to my father's place. He'll give you all the work you need. He's a retired lawyer and lacks any skill whatsoever with tools and such. He'll be glad of the help."

The loving pat on his shoulder from Isobela as she put his coffee mug in front of him spoke of her thanks, and Pedro's beaming face as he climbed onto his father's lap made his momentary loss of brain function worthwhile.

Now he'd done it! He'd be forced to go and see

his old man and face the past he'd ignored so long. Just the thought of opening those wounds made him feel ill.

***

Liam saw the curtains move as he and Ruiz approached the sidewalk of the sprawling, oversized rancher where he'd grown up. Before he could ring the bell, the door opened and his father stood in front of him, a huge smile of greeting plastered across his face.

Liam felt the discomfort immediately and would have given anything not to be here, not to face the one person who ranked highest on his list of people he didn't want to talk to or be near.

Close up, the old guy didn't look too good. For a man whose appearance had always been polished and debonair, he appeared scruffy and unkempt, his pants and shirt clean but wrinkled and his hair shaggy. Mind you, the gladness spread over his two-day bearded face made up for everything else... or at least it should have. But old hurts didn't just disappear—or even fade over time. Not if they'd been nursed.

"Liam!" How could a name ring with so much love? Discomforted, Liam stuck his hand out in a formal way and stepped into the hallway his father presented with a flourish.

He had trouble getting his feet to work; they wanted to run in the opposite direction, most likely because his brain was screaming for him to get the hell out of the place where he'd known such unhappiness, and where he'd sworn to never return.

"Hi, Dad." His father held his hand with both of his and wouldn't let go until Liam nodded to Ruiz and said, "I'd like you to meet Angelo Ruiz, a friend of mine."

Quickly the older man reached out to shake hands. "Welcome, Angelo. Any friend of Liam's is welcome in this house. Come into the garden with me, and I'll make coffee. By the way, my name is Paul."

As Liam followed behind the other two, he scanned the rest of the house to find it in a terrible mess. As they passed the kitchen, he glanced in to find it was the worst. Dishes were everywhere; the floor needed a good clean, and the smell of burnt food lingered to add a sourness that made his nostrils react. Whew! Not good!

The patio area was altogether a different story. The various reds and lush pinks abounding from the potted geraniums were beautiful, and the table clean. An opened newspaper lay next to a cup of steaming coffee and a small plate with toast crusts. A little idiosyncrasy of his dad's that Liam remembered. In fact, it would drive his mother into one of her numerous tirades, and to stop that from happening, Liam had taken to eating them himself just to stop the screaming—a secret he and his dad had shared. Now that she was no longer alive, who cared if they got eaten by a man or the nearby noisy birds?

Once they sat, coffee in front of each man, Paul made small talk with Angelo while Liam dealt with his inner conflicts. His guts hurt, and he needed a headache tablet. Automatically, he massaged his stomach until he spotted his dad's gaze riveted to his hand and he stopped instantly. Old eagle eye never did miss a thing.

Strange how any minute now, he expected to see his mom ranting at them from the doorway and, as was usual, sarcastically reaming out his dad. If he concentrated, he could hear again the woman's vitriol that had made him lose all respect for the man he couldn't help loving.

Anger rose just as it always did when he let himself remember. Following the anger was the shame that burned in his soul. Shame for loving his mother and hating his father's wife.

Shaking it off wasn't easy, but he had something he needed to do, and do it he would. Breaking into the others' conversation, he said in a firm voice, "Dad, this place is too much for you. You need help. And Angelo here needs a job. I thought we could work something out so you'd both benefit."

A pin could have dropped and been heard in the silence that only a slight breeze disturbed. First his dad looked at him, mouth open and eyes blinking rapidly. Then he turned a questioning glance to Angelo, whose hands white-knuckled the arms of his chair.

"You think I need some help here, son? I do believe you're right. Mrs. Brown passed away over a year ago, and I haven't been able to organize myself into finding another housekeeper or someone to look after the gardens. As you know, Mr. Brown used to look after the yard, but he moved into assisted living after she passed on."

"Angelo has a wife and two children, and they need a place to live. Is the apartment you built for me over the garage still free? It was roomy and had a separate entry. Maybe they could use that for a while."

"Sure they could. As you know it's furnished and needs a good clean, but I haven't disturbed anything since you left. If his wife doesn't mind, they're very welcome to the place. It would be wonderful for me to have company. The gardens are huge, and the kids will have lots of room to play."

Happiness is such a visual thing, thought Liam as he looked at his father. The old man had always been this way, every emotion plastered across his features and open to the world. Open to anyone who wanted to slap him down and walk all over him, take advantage of his good nature to the point of being brutal and mean and horrible. *Stop it! Don't go there!*

Plans were made, wages discussed, and arrangements organized for the family to move over in the next few days. Liam would rent a small truck and, between the three men, the move would happen.

"Can you stay for lunch?" Paul looked first at Angelo and then at Liam. The yearning on his face said it all. But his words had Liam checking his watch, and he jumped up from his chair and exclaimed, "Where the hell has the time gone? I have to go to work. Look, Angelo, I'll drop you off on my way, but we have to leave now."

Glad shock rang in his father's voice. "You're staying stateside? No more army? Son, I'm so... so glad."

"Nothing's been decided yet. I still have a few weeks." The harsh tone shouldn't have been used, and he regretted it as soon as he heard what he'd said and how. But he couldn't unsay it. That had always been the worst thing about hasty words. They couldn't be unsaid.

Chapter 15

Sadie stopped watching the traffic and finally broke the silence. "Liam, you're very quiet today. Are you mad that I called you on being late? Because if so, get over it. Pouting isn't at all manly. You knew that time was important in this job. If we get behind in the first run, the rest of the day is out of whack. You can shut off my babbling anytime you want to cut in."

The blank look he threw her way stopped her muttering. She realized her normally chatty companion had something on his mind, and her feminine instincts told her that he'd be better off talking about it than brooding.

"Don't take this as an open invitation, but if you need to talk about something, I'm a good listener." There, she decided. She'd said it plain out, and if he didn't take her up on her offer, then the heck with him. This man had used up far too much mind space already today—and last night too, if she was being honest.

Why he hadn't kissed her when she'd stood there with her lips all but flapping in front of his face as an offering, she'd never know. Rubbing noses was for kids, for heaven's sake. Yeah! But then why had it woken every rotten little sexual inclination in her body, all those aroused cells screaming at her all night long?

She looked up to see his cheeky grin, and relief flooded. He's back, she thought.

"You want me to tell you here, or can we take it to a couch? Like later in your apartment?"

"Like—not in this lifetime. You just looked... well, upset, and since we're friends... sort of... I thought I'd ask."

His voice lost its sassy note. Leaving one hand on the steering wheel, with the other he reached over to grasp her fingers. He squeezed them gently and said, "Thank you. I appreciate your caring—"

"Didn't say I cared."

"No, you didn't, but that's what friends do, right? They care. I care about you, and so you should care about me."

She pulled her fingers away and shrugged. "Fine, whatever. What's wrong?"

A grin slashed across his features, and she'd never seen him look more handsome, or so downright sexy. And this was the man who radiated sex like a Heatdish radiated heat.

"I'm worried about the baby."

If a heart could drop from its original location to the bottom of a stomach, then hers did. A baby! The asshole had a baby and never thought to tell her? The son-of-a-bi... She spit the words out before the screech got loose. "What baby?"

"Isobela Ruiz's baby. Oh, I never told you, did I? Later, on the day of the accident, I went back to visit them, to see if the boy Pedro had any repercussions from what happened, and I arrived in time to help the father, Angelo, while he delivered the baby. It was a girl. They called her Teresa." Strange, she'd swear she heard pride in his voice.

"You went back to visi...? I've been wanting to do that but didn't have the energy or the nerve. Figured I'd be intruding. But I worried about the boy. I'm so glad you did. That was really very thoughtful." She finally ran out like a cell phone whose battery power just ended. And this time, it was she who reached for his hand.

"Yeah, well, you saved him. It was me who hit him. A bit different. Plus you've been laid up some, and I haven't."

Awwww! He was trying to make her feel better. Maybe the hotshot wasn't such a jerk after all.

"Tell me about the baby. How did you just happen to get there in time for her birth? And what did you do?"

"You don't want to know. Suffice it to say, it seems to be my talent, lately. Being in the wrong place at the wrong time."

"So! Was she beautiful?"

"Who, the baby? Nope! She was wrinkly and red, and she screams a lot. Pedro's opinion not mine. But once she'd arrived, and this is my view, I thought her the most adorable female I'd ever laid eyes on."

By the sound of his voice, she figured he'd revisited those moments, and she could understand his sentiments. A baby's birth must be something to see.

Gosh, I'm an idiot, a flat-out bubblehead. Linking all males together. Look at Stan. He's really nice. And Liam's turning out to be a man I could admire. Maybe some guys aren't so bad. Sadie didn't know what to do with all the gushy feelings rampant inside her body. Urges smoldered. She wished she could throw her arms around his shoulders and squeeze.

And kiss him all over his face.

And rub her nose gently against his.

***

"He's gone! My baby's gone!"

"Mrs. Brill, calm down. Giorgio must have decided to take a walk or something like..." Nope. That didn't make sense. Sadie knew the dog hated walking. "Did you call the police?"

"Call the police? Pah! They didn't care. Asked

me few questions and then told me to check with the SPCA. I informed them that my Giorgio's worth was over $50,000 since he was an American champion for two years running, and you know what they said?"

Sadie shook her head, knowing the woman was on a roll. The flying spittle was only one of the clues. The wildness in her eyes another, and the biggest hint was the way she'd grabbed Sadie and shook her every time she spoke.

Intimidating, Liam stepped close, and the crazed lady had no choice but to let go and back away. Thank goodness, Sadie thought. Her arms were starting to feel numb. Which was a bit of an oxymoron if she ever heard one.

"They told me they had k-killers to find and drugs to get off the streets."

Her words broke through Sadie's distraction, and she zeroed back in time to see Liam catch Mrs. Brill just as she began to collapse. "My beautiful baby! How will he ever survive? All his precious things are here, his doggy bed, his special food, and the treats he loves..."

Before she could launch into another crying jag, Liam spoke harshly, snaring her attention.

"Show us where he was before he disappeared."

Swiping at her globby eyes with tissues that mysteriously appeared from inside her sleeve, she blew her nose, stiffened her backbone and said, "This way. I'll show you."

As they walked through the sumptuous apartment that had never been opened to her before, Sadie made out like a bobble doll—she couldn't see enough. What a palace! But way overdone for her taste, which didn't run to wine-colored velvet swag drapes and lavish carpeting to match.

Now the artwork? Well, that was a different matter altogether. She could have spent hours analyzing the picturesque landscapes and family portraits.

"Here." Mrs. Brill pointed to the luxurious patio enclosure with tall jungle-like plants, wonderful cascading flower baskets, and a plush mat that surrounded an enclosure which resembled a miniature castle. Oh, my god, thought Sadie. This was Giorgio's doghouse? At least she had the class to keep her thoughts to herself. Not so Liam.

"That's his doghouse?" Shock vibrated in his loud voice.

"Yes, I had it specially designed for him. He liked to come and lay in the sun sometimes, but I worried about his skin. He did use this house from time to time. Mostly, when he slept, he stayed near me. Which is why I'm so upset. I went to Greta's to get my hair done earlier, and my housekeeper had to go to the pharmacy to pick up some prescriptions. Giorgio refused to go along. Poor baby doesn't have a lot of energy left after his walks everyday. So, she left him here on the patio, as we do occasionally. But when she returned, he'd disappeared. We've looked everywhere." Tears gushed as soon as she'd finished her explanation.

Liam jerked his head at Sadie, and she knew he wanted out. With a heartfelt hug for the distraught woman, Sadie started towards the door. At the entrance, she stopped.

"Mrs. Brill, I have a few good shots of Giorgio that I can post around the neighborhood, and I'll warn the store owners that he's missing. Also, when I pick up my other dogs today, I'll pass out the word to their owners to take extra precautions with their own animals and to keep an eye open for him. If you hear anything at all, please let me know." Before she stepped out, from the corner of her eye she watched as Liam patted the old dear's shoulder, grinned one-sidedly, and left her trying to smile.

This guy was getting to her... digging his way through her walls of resistance. If she didn't want her heart broken, she'd better take care. After all, she'd only known him a short time. But then why did it feel as if she'd known him forever?

As he helped her back into the van, he swore. "Bastards! Stealing someone's pet. Should be shot."

"A little drastic, but I know what you mean. Giorgio's all she has, no children and no other interests, just the dog shows. I guess you could say he's her whole life." Sadie bit her lip to stop nattering as she tended to do when emotional.

"Has this ever happened before?"

"You mean dogs being stolen? Sure, especially these dogs. Most of them are worth a bundle. And they have to be untouched in order to be allowed into the conformation dog shows."

"Untouched?"

"Not spayed or neutered."

"Gotcha. I guess it makes sense. They're probably used for breeding purposes."

"Exactly. As Mrs. Brill explained, Giorgio himself is worth a lot of money, but his puppies would be worth a fortune. Not for showing, because they'd have to be registered, but there are people who don't care about the shows. They just want bragging rights. If only there was someone who might have seen what happened."

"Even though the patio is ground floor, I didn't notice any neighboring windows overlooking the space. It's pretty private."

"No help there, then. I'm going to ask around, Liam. Just the thought of some thieving jerks ripping off these people makes me want to scream."

"I might know of someone who could help. No promises, but he does have unusual powers of... of perception." He turned and held up his finger just as she intended to pose the next obvious question. "Don't ask!"

Chapter 16

Two more dogs were missing. As they went from place to place to pick up their brood, the story was the same and had Liam scratching his head. The common denominator happened to be obvious. They all lived within a mile of each other, in the rich district with homes where every dog's worth more than tripled the norm.

"Nicky? How in the world did they capture him? He hates men and wouldn't let a stranger anywhere near him. I don't get it." Sadie had become more upset with each dog-napping tale. Their day's schedule had to be re-organized, and as she worked the cell phone to call her clients, he saw her hands shaking.

Poor doll! He hated to see her so distressed, but he couldn't do anything until he contacted his mysterious apparition, who seemed to always be around when he didn't need him and disappeared during times when he could use his help.

"No!" Shock took over her voice as she spoke into the phone.

Liam pulled over to the side of the street and shoved the gearshift into park. "What?" As he watched Sadie's eyes fill, he felt like a size eleven had just kicked him in the guts. "Breathe. Stop crying. Tell me."

"Peppi! They took Peppi, my favorite of the bunch. He's such a little trooper, and so affectionate."

"Affectionate? He's a sugar-cube. Licked me all over when I finally caught up with him the other day." He used sarcasm on purpose to coax a smile, and it worked.

"I know he likes to run away, but he's the smartest of the bunch. Learned how to count before the rest, and will fetch anything I throw for him. Oh, Liam. Will we ever see them again? What do people do with stolen dogs? Where do they take them?"

"Logic tells me that they either sell them or use them for breeding—like in puppy mills."

"How horrible! Last night Stan, you remember Greta's boyfriend, mentioned that he was a cop. Do you think he might be able to help us solve this mystery, or at least give us some direction on where to start?"

He coughed, and then prattled on as though he

were in a sit-com trying to draw a laugh. "Oh, good idea! Now why didn't I think of him?"

"I get it!" She chuckled. "That was who you had in mind earlier. I'll call her and make arrangements for after work, see if they're free. Maybe we can order in pizzas and discuss it over dinner?"

"Great. In the meantime, we'd better walk the rest of your mutts."

She scrutinized his smile and eventually returned it. Glad to be able to ease her spirit without having to go into explanations, he breathed a sigh of relief. After all, how could a guy tell the girl who'd begun to mean way too much that he intended to pick the brains of his elusive guardian angel?

At their next stop, Liam waited in the van while Sadie approached the owner who stood at the gate with the dog sitting at the end of its flashy leash.

"Hey, Johnny? Angel? If you're hovering around I'd appreciate a moment."

"Hello, Mate. Just having a bit of a nap, I was. What can I do for you?"

Sure enough, there was the spitting image of Johnny Depp lounging in the back seat, head bolstered on his hand, elbow resting on the window edge.

"Sorry to disturb you." Liam could do sarcasm so well.

Shrugging nonchalantly, the angel yawned and answered, *"You're having me on, right?"*

Liam let his sigh last longer than usual and figured even an angel would get it. And it seemed he was right, by the cheeky grin he picked up through the rearview mirror.

"You want to know about the puppies?"

"Yes. The owners aren't the only ones upset with their disappearance. Sadie is heartbroken, and I want to help. Only I have no idea where to start."

As the phantom started to fade, he left behind the message, *"Stan is your man. He can find out what you need to know. And Liam, your first guess was right about puppy mills. And Oklahoma is a puppy mill Mecca. One more thing... follow the money."*

Just then Sadie approached the back door and waited for Liam to come and help her settle the golden retriever in his doggy seat. "Who were you talking to?"

"Me? I wasn't talking to anyone." Damn if his cheeks didn't feel hot.

"Oh, I get it! You're one of those weirdoes who carry on conversations with themselves." She giggled, and he loved the sound.

"You got me!" He winked in the wicked way he knew turned the girls on, guided her to her seat, and helped her inside.

***

"So you think there's a dog-theft ring branching out all over the city?"

Stan finished chewing his pizza and nodded. "Sure, we've been on to them for a while but haven't been able to find out where they're taking the dogs. As you know, the police department doesn't get involved with this type of crime as much as we'd like to. There just isn't enough manpower. But when it comes to the elite victims who've been hit recently, we've had to give up some time and start digging."

Sadie, who listened to every word, spoke up before Liam. "And, what did they find?"

"We think it's the Bradford brothers, mean-hearted sons of bitches—s'cuse my language—who are behind it all. They have high-class puppy boutiques and sell to the very rich. Unfortunately, whenever the S.P.C.A. searched their breeding premises, everything seems in order. The dogs look well cared for and healthy, with veterinarians available and all their papers up to date." He stood to get another glass of wine, then returned to his seat and carried on with his explanation.

"Thing is—they have a never-ending supply of puppies. Must be from outside this state. And we can't get the other officials to care very much about following up on that paperwork. The local humane society has helped some, but they can't trespass and so their hands are tied. Let me tell you, it's damn frustrating."

Liam asked, "If you knew which state to look in, would it help?"

"Depends on their laws. Why? Do you have an idea?"

"Oklahoma."

"Man! That would be the worst possibility. It's the perfect location for dishonest dog breeders. Without proper state regulations, they're rampant with puppy mills. What made you select that area?"

"Just a bit of info I picked up from a friend who had some inside knowledge. He said to follow the money."

Stan's expression took on a look of interest. He pulled out his cell, got to his feet, and excused himself.

Liam checked Sadie to see how she was taking in the disturbing discussion. She looked so downhearted. An ache began forming in his chest and promised to choke him if he didn't do something.

Greta shot him a wink and rose to clear the table. "I think we'll leave you guys now, cause Hotshot promised to take me to a movie tonight and it's my turn to choose. Chick flick, here we come."

As Stan flipped his phone closed, she slipped her arm through his and led him towards the back door.

"Whaddaya mean chick flick? No way!" He stopped and turned to where Liam and Sadie lounged on the couch. "I'll get back to you if I hear anything."

As soon as the bickerers closed the patio screen, Liam gently slapped at Sadie's hand to stop her picking at the pepperoni left on the piece of pizza she'd nearly demolished without eating a bite. She threw it onto the plate and set the plate on the table, then leaned back.

All he had to do was turn his head. Her face was so close he could feel her breath. He did so, but slowly, so as not to scare her. Then he watched as her eyes grew larger in the most beautiful face he'd ever seen. Expecting her to move away, he was glad when she didn't. But he could have sworn she'd turned to stone. Not a flicker, or a blink, nothing.

Earlier, he'd noticed that for once she'd used some kind of fancy pins to control her hair, but he didn't like to see the golden curls pulled back and squashed. Angling his fingers, he plucked them out and watched the mass settle around her rosy cheeks. She still hadn't moved.

Then he reached over and slid his hands underneath the softness and caressed her neck. Her eyes closed and a sigh of pure bliss escaped while he manipulated. Her muscles slackened and her body became limp under his ministrations.

This time, he couldn't pull away without tasting her. His body had already given him hell for the last trick he'd pulled. He'd had no sleep and no reprieve from imagining how she'd taste. Well he was about to find out.

***

God, the man was dense. Would he never get to it? Sadie didn't know how much longer she could hold out without mewing like a cat in heat. His lips were so close that his hot breath inflamed her already scattered senses.

His first touch released the moan and that seemed to act like a signal. One moment she was angled toward him while he held her head cradled in his big, gentle hands, and the next he'd whipped her around and she was lying across his body while his lips drained every spark of life-giving breath out of her.

Somehow she'd known he'd be able to kiss. That he'd be well versed in that particular method of seduction. But what he did to her went way beyond anything she could ever imagine. She was on fire. Throughout her body, heat scorched like a flamethrower gone berserk and then pooled between her legs—wet, devastating heat. Heat that turned her bones to mush and had her moving restlessly, seeking, aching for release from the ecstasy he'd started. One thing was for certain; whatever the devil wanted to do to her, she was ready and more than willing.

The first touch of his hands on her skin and her thoughts screamed "halleluiah." Then he stroked his way to where her breasts peaked and cupped her fullness. It felt wonderful. The warmth of his fingers caressing, plucking, and then caressing again forced more of those distracting explosions down below.

All the while he touched, he also kissed, and she found it difficult to concentrate on his lips.

He'd changed from tongue-in-mouth plundering to soft, lip-biting, tongue-sucking torment. She loved it. When his lips moved to her neck and her t-shirt got in the way, she was more than happy to help him remove the obstruction. And when he took off her bra, it only seemed sensible.

Snuggled back against his rapidly moving chest and hearing the ragged sighs he couldn't hide, she became aware that their passion affected him just as strongly. *I'm getting to him. Good!*

Just knowing he was equally affected gave her the strength to pull back and undo the buttons on his shirt. She glanced up to see him watching her fingers and then he looked right at her. Hot pools of lust had always seemed such a corny phrase in a trashy novel, but it described the look in his eyes perfectly. Her fingers stopped, and so did her heart.

His didn't. It vibrated. It actually moved around in the pocket that her hand lay against. A frustrated moan broke through her daze as he reached under her fingers to pull out his cell. Torn from her trance, her head flopped forward, and if the scream she heard inside could be let loose, he'd have a fairly good idea of just how demented she felt.

"It's Angelo. I have to answer it," he said in a harsh whisper, as he cradled her body by wrapping one arm around her and rubbing her back. He listened for a few seconds and then spoke the words that put paid to Sadie's fantasies.

"We'll be right there." He stabbed the off button and threw it on the coffee table. The sound of it slamming on the wooden surface somehow gave her a bit of satisfaction. It was a slight indication that he was as pissed off at the interruption as she was.

"There's something wrong with Angelo Ruiz's baby. He says she hasn't stopped crying for more than twenty minutes since her birth. Now Isobela has started, and he's at his wit's end. Can you call your mom? See if she'll be willing to check things out? Tell her we'll pick her up on the way."

Chapter 17

"She's hungry." Bea's diagnosis rang in the silence. Everyone had waited in fearful anticipation, hoping that the situation could be resolved without ambulances and a visit to the nearest hospital. For Sadie, hearing those words brought a strange relief, but it was also a sad testimonial.

"*Mío Díos*, no! I've fed her over and over. She spits my body out and doesn't want the milk. She won't eat. She won't sleep. She cries and cries—" The woman looked like hell and anguish rang in her voice.

"Isobela, trust me. It isn't your fault." Bea turned to the nearest person, who happened to be Liam, and unloaded the squalling baby into his arms before he could step back.

The fear on his face was a thing to behold and tickled Sadie's funny bone. Until he tried to pass the baby on to her. *Not in this lifetime!* She help up her hands and backed away. Her baby skills weren't any better than his. Finally he lifted the hysterical bundle against his shoulder, and began to whisper. Whatever he said worked like a magic chant. The crying eased and the hiccupping sobs slowed.

Bea's soothing voice drew Sadie's attention back to where the melodrama unfolded. The older woman held both the mother's trembling hands. "Isobela, have you been under a lot of stress lately? Maybe not sleeping or eating correctly, drinking too much coffee, or doing a lot of worrying? All this can affect your milk. Your body's production depends on how you treat it, and if you're tired and upset, things stop working properly."

Isobela, who stood clasped in Angelo's arms, lifted her face from his shoulder and stopped sniffling to listen. "This is true? It can be that my milk isn't good?"

"Oh, trust me; your milk is good, but not nourishing enough right now. She needs more."

Bea turned to Liam, who held the now miraculously quiet baby like she was a bundle of hot coals. "Liam, can you take Angelo and go to the drugstore for some baby formula?"

Isobela spoke up, her voice tremulous, her face lit with hope. "I have no bottles. You need to buy Teresa a bottle, also."

Liam forced the baby into Sadie's reluctant arms with a satisfied grin and motioned to Angelo.

Within a few seconds they were gone.

An instinct, from somewhere deep inside her female psyche emerged, and unaware of doing so, Sadie began to rock the baby, swaying from side to side. The squirming that had started as soon as Liam had abandoned the tiny mite vanished as she settled down once again.

Pedro, who had been peeking around the door from another room, crept from his hiding place and called to his mother.

"*Mamá?*"

"*Si, hijo.* You come visit with the ladies, but when papa returns, you must go back to bed."

Dressed in too short, too tight teddy-bear pajamas, he ran full tilt towards her, and she picked him up and squeezed him gently.

"What is wrong with our baby?" His chubby little hands seized his mother's cheeks, and his intent look meant business.

"Your sister is hungry. That is why she makes so much noise with her screaming. Your papa has gone with *Señor* Liam to buy her special food."

"Poor Teresa." His little hand reached towards the babe as if he wanted to stroke her, and so Sadie moved forwards to let him. Watching the touching scene unfold made it extremely difficult for her to swallow. The gentle way the boy patted his sister's blanket and the anxious tenderness obvious in his big brown eyes illustrated to her that this small family operated with love at its core.

"*Señora* Bea? Once she drinks the formula, will she still need my milk? I-I want to feed my baby like I did with Pedro. Breast-feeding is special for me, and it would break my heart if I couldn't do so any more."

"Oh, yes, my dear. Your milk is still more nourishing than anything bought in a grocery store. Besides, it's important for your body to keep the milk flowing. Just give her the formula as a supplement, so she feels full."

Bea wrapped an arm around the woman's shoulders. "Isobela, you must take care of yourself. You need to sleep. From the bags under your eyes, and those black circles, you haven't had a good rest in days. And you need to eat more protein and drink a lot—milk, juices, and water. If you follow these rules, very soon you'll see her settle down and be a happy, contented baby."

"I will do so, I promise. I've been so worried, but now, thanks to *Señor* Liam, my worries are over."

Bea—being Bea—couldn't help herself, and Sadie knew it. She wasn't at all surprised when her mother asked the question. *Thank you, Mom!*

"What did Liam do to help?"

"He has found my Angelo a job and our family a place to live. We are to look after his father and take care of the house and gardens. And we get to move this weekend and leave this horrible place."

"You'll live in the house with his family?"

"He has only a father. Angelo thinks maybe his

mother has passed on." Isobela made the sign of the cross and then continued, "According to what he told me, they showed him a beautiful apartment which will be our new home. It is attached to the garage. I can't tell you how blessed we feel to have such a friend as *Don* Liam."

Pedro piped up and added, "There's a garden for me to play, and lots of grass. And an old man who will maybe be my friend."

"If you behave like a good boy." His mother smoothed his curls.

"I will be the best good boy, *Mamá*. I promise."

Sadie fell in love with the little man all over again. She felt the muscles in her throat tighten from hearing the happiness in his voice. Swallowing became difficult, and she had to speak low so as not to wake the now sleeping baby.

"He'll love you, kiddo. He won't be able to help himself."

Bea nodded and agreed. "I just met you, and already you're my hero." She laughed when Pedro grinned and hid his face against his mother's neck. Then she turned to Sadie. "That look suits you, my love."

Sadie backed away. "Don't get any ideas." Her touchiness belied her true feelings. Watching the tiny face between the folds of the soft, blue, well-worn blanket had instigated the most unique flow of emotions she'd ever experienced.

Visions of a different baby, Liam's baby, with his

features and his dimples, evoked tingles of pleasure that started in her tummy and strangely made her knees feel weak.

***

While driving, Liam glanced into the rearview mirror and teased Bea in the back seat. "Thank you for your kindness tonight, Miss Nightingale. It was really appreciated. The Ruiz family has no money, and they fear doctors since they're here illegally. I hoped your nursing knowledge would be enough to help them."

Bea, surrounded by her black bag and her huge purse, smiled. "Teresa's basically healthy and seems well-cared for. So is their little boy. Therefore I knew they weren't being neglected. There had to be another reason for the baby's symptoms."

"They're good people."

"As you guaranteed earlier. It's not Isobela's fault that her milk hasn't enough sustenance to nourish the baby. I'm glad you explained how stressful things have been for them lately. It did help me in my prognosis. Isobela needs to sleep and let her body become stronger. Birthing is traumatic; it takes a lot out of a female's constitution."

His voice droll, Liam added, "Not so easy on the old man, either."

Bea chuckled in sympathy. While the men had gone to get the formula, Isobela had shared her experience with the women about Teresa's birth. In fact they'd had a bit of a giggle after listening to her graphic details.

"Once they get settled in their new home, and she has the benefit of some good wholesome food, she'll be just fine. Speaking of good food, what time do you want me and the girls to pick you up tomorrow, Sadie?"

Sadie turned to look into the back seat. "Why? Where are we going?" She knew her voice came out sharper than she'd intended, but being shocked out of her fantasy world of picking up with Liam from where they'd left off earlier, she hadn't taken the time to filter her attitude.

"To the lake, remember? You promised! We want to get an early start. Is that a problem for you? I've got all the food and necessities organized, so all you need to do is bring a swimsuit and a change of clothes."

"Aw, Mom. I totally forgot, and I—"

"Uh-huh, Sadie. You don't get to back out at this late date. We've all been looking forward so much to having family time. The girls downloaded two of the top romantic comedies, I baked and cooked all your favorites, and we've loaded up on all the good junk food. It'll be a blast, sweetheart."

"Sounds wonderful! Don't know how you can refuse." Liam grinned wickedly in her direction, and under cover of darkness, she pinched his side. Hard! Heard the expletive and felt some satisfaction. *Turncoat!*

They pulled up in front of the house, and Bea leaned over the seat to give Sadie an awkward hug. She squeezed Liam's shoulder in farewell and opened the car door. Before she could step out, Liam had made his way to her side and leaned in to offer his hand.

"You are one sweet man, Liam. If I weren't old enough to be your mother, I'd lasso and corral you."

"Hey, I like older women." He kept her hand as he led her up the front walk, her bags tucked safely under his free arm.

Once they approached the door, Bea passed him a card and whispered in a voice only he could hear, "Here's the address and phone number of where we'll be for the next two days. If you were to show up Sunday morning to rescue Sadie before she loses her mind, I know she'd be thankful. Never underestimate how far a crazed girl might be willing to go in payment for such a sensitive deed, my lad."

"The heck with Sadie. How about you and me getting it on? You're just my kind of chick."

Sadie flinched at the loudness of her mother's bellowing laughter and shook her head when she heard Liam join in. One was just as bad as the other. But the warm glow that started in her body couldn't be stopped, and so she let it fill her and erase the pissy feeling she'd gotten when her mother had reminded her of her earlier promise.

Visions of spending the night with Liam wilted and died. Her hands clenched as she crossed her legs and tightened the throbbing areas in her lower half that had dared to anticipate a glorious night of celebrating her newly awakened libido.

Chapter 18

After dropping Sadie at her house with a light embrace and a friendly kind of kiss, Liam took his unsatisfied body, still aching from the earlier disappointments, and escaped temptation as fast as he could without looking too much like an asshole.

Before Bea had warned Sadie of their early-morning plans, he'd envisioned them returning to her place and spending the night wrapped around each other.

But family couldn't and shouldn't be ignored. The thought of coming between Sadie and her mother and sisters wasn't on the table. Look at his relationship with his own father. Growing up he never knew whom he hated worse. The shrew of a mother who could turn from a sweetheart to a bitch at the drop of a hat, or the man who let her use him as her personal whipping boy.

To this day he was screwed up because of these sentiments. Having already sensed elements of unease when Sadie passed time with her family, he also understood that she loved them dearly and would never hurt them. He envied her that kind of relationship and would honor it.

Enough! Out from under her spell, he could think more clearly. He knew he needed to stop fixating about a girl he had no right to care for! Ruiz's call had come at a fortuitous moment. And he knew just who to thank for that happening.

Earlier, while shopping, the two men had talked and Ruiz had explained how Liam's name had come to his mind as if sent from some force that wouldn't let up until he'd placed the call. No doubt about it—Johnny-come-lately working his magic. Guess he owed him his thanks. With his life in such a mess, Liam knew he'd best concentrate on how the hell he'd be able to once again have a full night's sleep.

Too bad tonight wasn't the night. Wide awake, he pulled to the side of the road and reached for the iPad he carried in a special pouch in his car. Scrolling through the Internet, he did a search on the Bradford brothers. In no time at all, he had a fairly good idea of the scope of these two men, where they lived, their business background and associates.

Since he knew there'd be no rest for him that night, he decided to do a drive-by and survey their fancy pet store where they sold a huge variety of dog breeds. Advertised as the best, he'd noticed the quality of the photographs on their distinctive website. Those had to have been taken by a professional. In fact, the whole enterprise looked to be uniquely expensive.

Certain the culprits would never keep the newly stolen dogs in so inappropriate a place, nonetheless he felt it imperative to get a good feel for what he and Sadie were up against.

The night warranted putting the top down and he drove along happily, letting the warm breeze cool the heat still rampaging inside his body. As he passed near the Potomac River, he spotted the glorious Lincoln Memorial ablaze with lights, glowing as a reminder that his country had fought and won the battle for freedom and Independence. Just like the battles he fought with his conscience every night... *Hey, man! Don't go there!*

He shook off the waiting depression and realized it had been easier. With so much on his mind, he hadn't had time to dwell and smolder in all that pain. Maybe the shrink was right.

No! Staying busy helped, but a man had to relax sooner or later. And if every time he closed his eyes, he saw bloodshed and horror, then it wasn't getting better.

The honking behind hurled him from the sickening memories and made him pay attention to his driving.

The ostentatious building that housed the pet store stood amongst other buildings full of designer-like commodities—a fancy shoe store on one side and a jewelry boutique on the other.

Leaving the car, Liam made his way over to glance into the window, not surprised to see that fancy wooden blinds closed off the view of the inside. He wandered over to the other side of the building and noticed there was a narrow walkway that led to the back. Glancing each way first to see if anyone paid attention; he skulked forward and made his way under a lit window.

High up on the brick wall, the ledge poked out some three or four inches, enough that he could use it to chin up in order to briefly see inside.

Three men sat around a luxurious office of brown leather, crystal artifacts, and dark wooden bookshelves. They all held drinks and a tray with a decanter sat on the low table in front of them.

Anchoring himself with one arm, Liam reached for his cell phone and, using the video feature, panned the room and then zeroed in on all three men. By this time his muscles were screaming.

Liam wished he could read lips. Not a sound came through the double-paned glass, so he had no idea what was being discussed. From the celebratory way they'd clinked glasses, he had no doubt these three dudes were happy about something. And he couldn't help but wonder if the missing dogs had anything to do with their contentment.

Just before he lowered himself, the three stood up and shook hands. Back on his feet, he meandered to the sidewalk, trying to look inconspicuous, and then headed for his convertible. To put the top up took only a few seconds but gave him a reason for being parked there, and the men who all left the store together didn't even look his way.

Head lowered, he snuck glances and saw that two of the men stood side by side as if a team, while the other backed away first. He now knew which ones were the Bradford brothers. Dressed in expensive suits with ties to match their shirts, carrying brimming briefcases, they stood shoulder to shoulder, the same height. And both were partially bald, slim built, and wore glasses.

Having just read their resumes, he knew they lived on the same property, in separate houses. Talk about togetherness. How ridiculous!

Their Lincoln SUV wasn't hard to follow, since they had chosen white with all the bells and whistles. Then again, the cheesy lit-up license plate reading I "heart" Dogs would have kept him on track anyway.

Sure enough, they drove to their property, where the gate swung open to let them enter. Liam just kept driving along and didn't pull up until a block later. He'd done everything he could tonight. If he got the video to Stan early in the morning, before the scheduled move for the Ruiz family, he hoped the identity of the third man might give some clues to where Giorgio and the other missing pets were being held.

If nothing else, rather than just accept the inevitable; at least he'd tried to do something. Right now, there was so much going on in his life that he had no choice but to put up with. Damned if it wasn't making him sick inside. This crisis had chosen him, and he had no intentions of bowing out.

Seriously, how many times can a man back away before he breaks...?

Chapter 19

Sadie plodded around her place, dreading the coming trip. Knowing there wasn't a damn thing she could do to stop it from happening, she chose her least favorite swimsuit, a sexy, revealing number she knew would please her mother, and shoved it into her backpack. Then she whipped out a cute little sundress she'd gotten for her last birthday, one she'd never have bought herself but had to admit fit perfectly, and rolled it up to add to the rest. She grabbed the matching cardigan she'd worn a few days earlier and rolled it up, also.

Her plush towel, flip-flops, suntan lotion, and makeup bag were retrieved, and pretty soon she stood ready. Not willing, but ready. A check to her cell phone, hoping a text awaited her, had her pushing down the disappointment when the screen came up blank. She understood Liam had a lot to do this morning. They were moving Angelo and the family, and she shouldn't expect any calls or messages. She knew that in her head, but her stupid heart wasn't as reasonable.

The honking, loud and typical, made her run to the door. Trust her mother to forget that people liked to sleep in on the weekends.

"Hi, baby. Are you ready for a great time?" Bea's floppy hat shielded her eyes and had Sadie wondering if she could even see the road. Next to her mother, the shotgun seat waited—empty. Sadie knew her other two sisters, both of whom were grinning impudently from the back with an ecstatic, tail-waving Susie nestled between them, were fully aware of the unwanted honor of sitting in the front. The foolish woman collected tickets for traffic violations without any qualms whatsoever. And on the two-hour drive they were sure to be stopped at least once.

Knowing there was no escape; Sadie stuffed her backpack as best she could into the jam-packed trunk and then settled into the low front seat. Desultory topics floated around her, of course in the screamy tones she was used to, but she let their voices lull her into a delicious daydream where Liam had actually stayed with her the night before. Their banter finally broke into her trance and made her aware of her surroundings.

Warmth from the sun settled her nerves, and she started to look forward to their time at Lake

Anna. Balmy weather and beautiful scenery helped soothe, also. Reminiscences of their cozy cabin, which had made many of the summers worth living in her youth, had her anticipation growing. Relaxing against the leather seat, she breathed in the fragrance of various perfumes that radiated around the happy females of her zany family.

Her mother stuck in a CD and "Rolling in the Deep" belted out in Adele's brilliant voice compelled her to hum softly. The song, one of her all-time favorites, made her feel strangely happy. No doubt it was the catchy beat.

And then the worst happened... when the agony really began. Three voices joined in, along with one happy hound dog, all harmonizing to destroy not only the tune but the great lyrics. Cows being tortured couldn't sound worse. *No! Lord, this isn't fair. I'm a good person...*

By the time they arrived at the cottage, Sadie thanked the gods she didn't have a gun. If the drive down was to be a reflection of the rest of her time with "the girls," she hoped they'd brought a lot of wine.

Chapter 20

Liam spoke softly. "Hey Dad, after we finish setting up Pedro's bed, can I have a moment?" All morning they'd been hard at work moving Alfonso and Isabel's meager belongings into the suite, and then transferring much-needed furniture from the big house to fill up the empty spaces. They were now busy finishing up the smaller chores.

A plan had come to Liam during his sleepless night, one where he'd need his father's help. Asking any favors from the old man wasn't easy for him, but the cause justified lowering his boundaries—and even begging, if necessary.

"Sure, son. I'm happy to help in any way I can. And while we have this time alone, I just want you to know how happy you've made this ol' guy by bringing the Ruiz family into my life. After your mom passed on, things got pretty tough. Retiring made the loneliness worse. Being stuck at home with no one to talk to and only my ugly mug to look at had me considering that selling might be an option—moving into a home, just to have company." He heaved a sigh. "I have to admit it would have broken my heart to give up this old house. As you know, it's been in our family for the last two generations, and hopefully, you'll want to take it over when the time comes."

Liam stiffened. He couldn't help it, and he knew his dad sensed he'd gone too far.

"Sorry, Liam. I wasn't trying to tie you to anything. Of course, it'll be your decision down the road. For now, I'll enjoy having the young company and the help to keep the house from falling down around our ears."

"Yeah, fine, Dad." Liam wished he'd shut the hell up, because with every word his father uttered, his own pain increased. Tension settled between his shoulder blades, and no amount of stretching could loosen the tightness. He'd left home because of this agony—the knowing that he'd never rise to his mother's high expectations or lower himself to his father's level.

Soon they were sharing a coffee in the garden after finishing all the chores. Isobela and Angelo were puttering happily in their new home, and the children were napping. Liam's heart had twisted in knots at the threadbare furniture and small amount of belongings they owned. Such nice people dealing with so much hardship—didn't seem right somehow. He shrugged and rolled his neck from side to side.

"You wanted me to help?" The soothing tone relaxed his anxieties, and the uncomfortable moment passed.

"If you don't mind, I need you to dress in one of your expensive lawyer suits and come puppy shopping with me. There's a fancy doggy boutique downtown, and I want to get inside and see how they handle customers. I'm especially interested in their sales procedures and the commitments they might make to a promising customer.

"You're talking about a pet shop, right?" His father seemed perplexed.

"There's a little more to it than that. This is a high-class, very expensive pet shop. And I need to understand their policies and the guarantees they're willing to give as to the breeding of their animals. Whether or not they can promise champion sires and mothers of the same quality. You see, Sadie, a friend of mine, is a dog-walker for a very elite group here in Washington, and some of her best dogs were stolen recently. These weren't ordinary mutts. Most of their price tags ranged in the thousands and tens of thousands of dollars."

"Imagine that! But then I've never given it much thought. You say you want me to go and buy one of these dogs?"

"No, not buy. Just enquire while I snoop around

a little."

"Sure, I can do that. When did you want to leave?"

"How about after lunch?"

***

Watching the Ruiz family as they settled into their new home made Liam's sacrifices all seem worthwhile. He liked seeing Pedro run around the same yard that had amazed him as a little boy. The pond full of goldfish drew the child like it had always drawn him.

His father had attached a new rope swing where his old one used to hang, and if the kid's excited giggling was anything to go by, it looked as if it would take first prize for his favorite new plaything. Excited, the little guy didn't know whether he was coming or going.

Isobela, with a satisfied Teresa nestled in a holder against her chest, beamed at everyone. He'd watched her hug Alfonso more than once as if in wonder at their good tidings. Even he'd gotten an embrace when he introduced her to her new place, the apartment his mother had contracted and decorated for him so he wouldn't leave home. As if that would've kept him in this hellhole!

Pretty soon, all the empty boxes and cartons were put in the garage and the yard was so well organized one would never have known that a move had taken place just a few hours earlier.

A quick bite to eat—sandwiches made by a

contented Isobela—and the time had come for him and his dad to leave.

They went into different rooms to change, his dad to the master suite and Liam, with his change of clothes, into his old bedroom—his retreat from what used to happen in other parts of the house. The fights, or rather his mother fighting and his dad taking her abuse, had been a constant nightmare.

A sour taste bombarded his mouth, and his stomach clenched like in the old days as he remembered the nights he'd fall asleep with his pillow held over his ears and his ragged teddy held in his arms. Later, as a teenager, earphones and loud music had soothed his troubled soul.

Just get the hell out of here, he told himself. No damn good to you now, remembering old times. They're done and gone. He dressed quickly and couldn't get downstairs fast enough.

Liam felt a pang as soon as his father appeared wearing the same kind of clothes he'd worn for as long as Liam could remember. An expensive dark suit, a silk tie worth hundreds, and shoes made with luxurious leather altered him from the retired crossword-puzzle enthusiast to the suave, high-priced lawyer he'd been his whole career. He'd even oiled back his hair to look less scruffy and more in keeping with the sharp image of a man at the top.

Guts twisting caught Liam off guard. Seeing his father looking so like his old self brought back memories he'd forgotten. The times his dad had put down his briefcase to go and help him fix his bike rather than leave for the office. Or when he'd sat on the stairs listening while his distraught son poured out his problems, or the many nights when he'd help with the homework young Liam couldn't understand. Even when a girl had kissed him by the lockers and he hadn't known how to handle it, what to say to her or what she expected, the ol' man had been there for him. How could he have forgotten?

He knew how. His mother's screams had drowned out the gentleness in his father's voice and his loving ways. And her belittling of her husband had lowered his stature in his son's all-seeing eyes.

"Will I pass muster, Liam?"

The anxious look on the familiar face seemed as if he'd been privy to Liam's thoughts. A wave of anguish travelled up his back and buried itself inside his already crowded head.

"Yeah, you look good." Liam held out his hand for the keys to the silver Mercedes parked in the driveway and grinned when his dad hesitated. Can't separate a man from his toys easily, he decided, knowing he'd have had difficulty giving up his convertible.

The store didn't look near as fancy from the outside as it did inside. Photographs of stunning dogs, posed like champions, decorated most of the walls. Pedigrees, ribbons and other types of memorabilia were highlighted in a featured glass enclosure and drew the customer like dust to a Swiffer. The gray carpets were plush and the wallpaper to match pricey. Everything screamed class and respectability and brought the hackles rising on Liam's neck.

These scumbags used the money from mistreated canines to live like this? He ached to bring them down. Maybe he didn't have the same love for Giorgio or Peppi as Sadie or their owners had, but he did hate the kind of men who used defenseless animals to feather their own nests. Bastards! Jail was too good for these guys, but since it was all they had, it was better than letting the assholes run around free to wreak their havoc and break hearts.

The man who approached them, sauntering as if he had all the time in the world, smiled and held out his hand.

"How can I help you? I'm Richard Bradford, part owner of the Palace of Pups. Are you looking to add to your family today?"

Slimy son of a bitch, Liam thought. The words were so practiced that not an ounce of sincerity rang through.

Playing the game, Liam and his father shook hands. Then Paul spoke. "Yes. I have a new family moving in with me who have a little boy about four years old. A pup running around the place would be the perfect playmate. A friend referred me here, and so I thought I'd come in and get some details on the type of animals you can offer."

Holy cow, the old man still had it in him, that urbane handling of other people—a good lawyer's trademark.

"Then you wouldn't be at all interested in putting the dog in shows in the future?"

"No, I don't think so. But of course, I'm only interested in a purebred with good family traits."

"Of course, Mister...?"

"Paul O'Brien, and this is my son, Liam."

"We like to pair our clients with a pup according to your specific requirements. In that way, you'll be confident in the predictability of the specific breed, and of course you can rest assured that each animal will be of the highest standard."

"I see. Yes, that sounds perfect. I guess we'll need a mild-mannered dog that loves children, has lots of energy, and is easy to train."

"Would you be looking for a guard dog?"

"Not specifically, but I'd hope it would have a natural instinct to guard, not only the boy but the house. And although this wouldn't be a main prerequisite, I can't stand dogs being too yappy, either."

A falsetto laugh grated on Liam's nerves. He wanted to break Bradford's face in order to stop the irritation.

"Come with me to the office, and I'll show you

photographs of the stock we have available at the moment."

Liam broke his silence and asked, "Is there any way we could pay a visit to where you have the dogs housed? I think it would be helpful for my dad to see not only the pups but the mothers and sires, also. I've read that if a potential owner wants a future glimpse of his pup, he should check out its parents."

"That's true if you're buying from an unlicensed breeder. We have only the best dogs in our stable and would give you a total guarantee of quality. Therefore, it wouldn't be necessary for you to have to do any traveling to the kennels. But we do have photographs of our farm, and I'll be glad to show you some of the features."

Liam watched the jerk walk like a sissy, and as he trailed behind, he wished he could give his sashaying ass a satisfying swift kick.

Settled into the leather seats in the upstairs office, Liam and Paul looked at each other, eyebrows raised in speculation. All the while their host busied himself gathering paperwork from his desk, he prattled on about the most popular breeds.

"Let me see now. We have Labs, Terriers, German Shepherds, Golden Retrievers, Poodles—one of our best sellers—the ladies do love their Poodles. And then there's Shih-tzus, Beagles, and we've just lately branched into

Pomeranians, since we've found a wonderful sire for our female."

That's it! I am gonna rip the guy's face off... Holding back wasn't sitting right with Liam's tense stomach or the threatening headache. Sure as hell, he'd be suffering later. Another sleepless night.

The degenerate smiled in his oily way and nestled into the seat across the table from where they sat. "Can I offer you coffee or a soft drink?" His affected gesture towards the mini kitchen was another reason for dislike.

"No thanks." Paul looked toward Liam, who shook his head. "We'd like to know more about your facilities, if you don't mind."

"Of course." He passed them a bundle of professionally done posters with amazing photographs of various animals. Some featured puppies, while the others showed only the female or male parents. At the end of the pile, an exact replica of Peppi's orange-brindled face stared back at Liam, and he had to stop himself from leaping across the low table and satisfying his need for revenge. He'd swear this was the little bugger who'd led him on a chase for three blocks and then washed his face all the way back.

"As I mentioned earlier, we've managed to add Pomeranians to our growing numbers. The male and female just came to us a short time ago, so it'll be some time before there'll be a litter. But I have no doubt we'll be offering the puppies soon."

"What do you have that's available right now? I wouldn't want to wait for too long." As he spoke, Paul sifted through the pile and stopped on one poster. "For instance, I see there are Golden Retriever puppies available?"

"Yes, the dam, Sunny Glow, has championship papers, and her breeding lines are impeccable. The sire, Golden Fellow, is also from one of the best kennels in the country and has many blue ribbons to prove his perfection in his class. Truly, this is an ideal choice for a companion for a small boy. These particular dogs are great for families, gentle and sweet natured. Not only that, they're beautiful to look at and intelligent, besides being the most sought after of all the dogs we own. I already had homes for all five pups in that poster, but one of the families, the ambassador for England no less, just notified me they'd been moving back home and so the little female in the middle is now available."

"What do you think, Liam? Do you like the look of these little bundles?"

Liam heard the yearning in his father's voice, and his internal antenna began to work overtime. Why the old fraud intended for this to be a real sale.

"Sure. But don't you want to consider other options before buying?"

"No, I don't think I do. So, Mr. Bradford, what's the price for this puppy, and when and where do I pick it up?"

Why the crafty devil! Now Liam understood his father's reasoning.

"You're very lucky, Mr. O'Brien. The pups have reached eight weeks old and are now ready leave their mother. With a guarantee, of course, that they're up-to-date with all their vaccinations. We like to bring the animals here to the pet shop for our new owners to collect. Because, added into the buying price, we have a fine selection of leashes and collars to choose from as our gift, plus there's a huge array of other accessories you might like to look over to help make the new member of your family feel truly at home."

"Do you at least have a brochure or a picture of your farm, where the puppies are raised? I have a lot of friends and associates who'll most likely be asking as soon as they see the puppy."

"Hum, yes, I do have a few shots we've taken of the farm. Let me get them for you. And I'll have my assistant organize your paperwork and receipt at the same time, shall I?"

"Yes. That will be fine. Hopefully you won't bankrupt me?" Paul joked, but with an edge that had the other man hesitate before he left the room.

"Quick, go through his desk, and I'll stay by the door." Paul motioned to Liam, who'd already moved in that direction.

First he picked up the cell phone left behind, and with a few clicks had the list of previous phone numbers revealed on the screen. He pulled out his own phone and carefully took a photo. Then he rifled through some loose sheets in the top drawer to see if there was anything incriminating. *Damn! Nothing!*

Just then a ping sounded in his mind, which made him look up to see his pirate friend standing beside the wooden file cabinet, arms crossed, legs splayed and an angry frown on his face.

"In the left side drawer. Hurry! Get the camera ready."

"Hey, nice of you to drop in. Long time no see!"

"Missed me, did ya?"

"Yeah, like a rash." Liam grinned at the cocky fellow that he was surprisingly glad to see.

"Hurry, the miserable little worm is coming back."

Sure enough, there was a copy of an e-mail dated today that said puppies would be arriving from the breeder in Oklahoma that evening, and the same vehicle would then transport the newest shipment of dogs from Bradford's place in the return trip.

That left them twenty-four hours to find the crummy farm. So much for his plans to go to the lake and see his girl! Probably just as well. He knew he had no business encouraging Sadie to fall in love with him—or vice versa. Right now his life was so screwed up, she'd be far better off with a guy who could sleep at night without waking up screaming.

A hissing sound brought his attention back to the matter at hand, and he quickly took a photo of the paper he held before placing it back where he'd found it and closing the drawer. There was only enough time to show his thumb to the now angelically smiling John-boy and move back towards his seat before he heard steps approaching.

A picture hanging on the nearest wall drew him like it had been magnetized. Acting nonchalant, he stopped to study it. It was a lovely landscape with a faint conglomeration of buildings and the view of a lake in the distance.

The door opened and Bradford stepped into the room, spied Liam by the watercolor, and moved to join him. "I see you're attracted to this painting. We commissioned it to be done of the... of some property we used to own," said Bradford, his tone full of pride as he stepped closer to Liam. "It was painted many years ago by Lara Schnell, who today is a very well-known artist. Art is a huge passion of my brother's; he spends a lot of time in galleries and even dabbles a bit himself." Bradford waved Liam toward his seat and stepped back to let him pass, the gesture saying in no uncertain terms that the subject was now closed.

Paul, pretending to study the posters from earlier, put them down and smiled convincingly at the slimeball whose greasy smirk had Liam's fists itching. He had to get out of this room before he blew the whole operation.

As if sensing his son's discomfort, Paul rose and looked at his watch, then stuck out his hand for the sheaf of papers held in his direction. "Oh, good, you have the paperwork."

Liam watched his father's expression as he perused each sheet and knew exactly when he'd come to their price. The raised eyebrows and cough made him slightly uncomfortable, but he watched as the old man carried it off without a glitch.

"Yes, this seems reasonable. I'll give you half now and pay the difference as soon as I take possession of the dog. I see here the puppy's kennel name is Luna Mist. That is lovely. I know she'll fit in with our family very well."

"I have no doubt; she is a purebred with an impeccable bloodline and worth every penny. I'm very happy we were able to be of service. We should have the pup ready to be picked up here in the store on Monday. I'll call you myself to let you know she's arrived."

Once the arrangements had been settled, Liam couldn't get out of the place fast enough. And he couldn't believe his father had gone so far as to buy the puppy.

Back in the car, he questioned the self-satisfied guy sitting next to him. "Why in the world did you actually give that asshole money? We agreed you would be making inquiries, nothing more."

Paul's discomfort showed as he squirmed and looked everywhere but at Liam. Finally he spoke. "When I was a lad, we always had dogs running around the place. But they terrified your mother, and she wouldn't even discuss the possibility. Not even as a pet for you. And you know how she'd bend the rules for her boy? But things are different now that she's at peace. I can go ahead and own a pet... and no doubt, the boy, Pedro, will enjoy having an extra playmate also. A win-win situation, right?"

Liam caught the self-satisfied smirk, and gladness filled him up and crowded out some of the blackness he couldn't seem to shake.

Chapter 21

"Dad, do you mind if I stop for a minute and use your landline to update Stan, a friend with the Metropolitan Police? My cell phone is getting low; hopefully I'll have enough juice to send the picture I took. If I try and talk also, my battery will be dead."

"Liam, you don't need to ask me. This is your home..." He held his hand up to stop Liam from interrupting. "I know it's my house. But, son, it was once and always will be your home." The words seemed to choke him up, and he quickly got out of the car. "Come on in. I'll organize some coffee while you make your calls. I noticed my cell phone is the same model as yours, so you can hook it up to my charger."

Once seated, facing each other, they re-hashed the afternoon's events and Liam brought his father up to date on what Stan had managed to uncover after Liam had sent him the information and photos from the night before.

"According to Stan, these guys have kept a very low profile. They'd rather pay others to do their dirty work for them. When expensive, high-quality animals suddenly show up and become available for sale or for breeding purposes, there's no questions asked. After all, they're in the business."

"The rotters!" Paul hadn't been a top-notch defense attorney without gaining a modicum of detachment, but Liam could literally see and feel his father's wrath. It made them seem connected, and that felt good.

"Yeah! You said it. Stan's been in touch with Washington's Humane Law Enforcement Department. They have nothing on these guys. But he said they're interested and would be more than willing to take the case to the U.S. Attorney's office if we can get the goods on this operation."

"That's great news."

"I know. When I sent him the list of calls just now, he sounded quite excited. Then I stumped him with the news that they're moving the animals from the farm tonight. Somehow we need to be there. He's pretty sure their main puppy mill would be in Oklahoma and so has been focusing his attention on anything linking them with that state. Shipping papers, border info, anything he can get his hands on that might give them any clues."

"If we only knew where the farm was located." Paul scratched the side of his face, a gesture Liam found so familiar.

"That would solve a lot of our problems." He knew it was the missing link, but right now they were whistling in the wind.

"Liam, remember when you stopped at the painting and Bradford said it was painted by Laura Schnell? She did move to New York recently, and he's right, she's become quite famous, her landscapes bring in top dollar. Anyway, I know he mentioned that it was property they used to own, but in case you didn't pick it up, he hesitated and corrected what he'd been about to say. To me it was a glaring 'tell' that he lied. If your friend, Stan, was to get in touch with this woman and ask her directions to the place, maybe the deed on that property could prove ownership and, well... you never know."

"I never thought about that—man, you are a genius!" Carried away by his enthusiasm, Liam added, "I'm proud to be your son."

The old saying that "Silence could be cut with a knife" fit the moment perfectly. Emotions rose, and the atmosphere became tense. Finally Liam moved to grab the phone once again and call in the goods to Stan.

As if that spontaneous remark had opened a path never to be ignored again, Paul sat and waited.

As soon as Liam had replaced the receiver, his father cleared his throat; the redness crawled up his neck.

"I can't tell you how wonderful it's been hanging out with you today, son."

God, don't do this to me. Not now! Liam knew his expression had darkened. When he heard those words, he felt the lights go off inside, and like a raging avalanche that can't be stopped, neither could his despair.

"Dad, I'd rather not talk about this now." When he leapt to his feet, he knocked some books off the coffee table and automatically bent over to pick them up. For a few seconds, panic and nausea attacked and left him breathless. So much so that it was all he could do to throw himself back onto the sofa and clutch his head. Pain blasted inside, and how he didn't pass out, he'd never know.

"Liam! What the hell's going on with you? If it's the army, you can always quit and finish your law degree."

"It's not that. Leave it alone, Dad."

"I can't. I've been watching you all day, and you're self-destructing. I've... I've had enough! Now you're going to tell me what's making you look like the devil is riding your coattails."

A head-on collision took place in his brain, his overwhelming need against his want to not go there. He spit the words from his mouth as if they were rotten. "It's the blasted nightmares. I can't sleep, and food tastes like crap. The only time I can forget is when I'm busy, and so I never stop staying busy."

"Something is behind this, Liam. It's not normal for a guy to be suffering these symptoms. Have you talked to a doctor?"

"Sure. All they've done is give me drugs and refer me to a shrink."

"What did the shrink say?"

"Didn't go. Dad, I'm not crazy. It's just I had to do some bad shit while overseas and it's been... well... haunting me."

"Like what kind of bad shit? Tell me, Liam. Don't go getting that stubborn look and shut down on me now. Just blurt it out. Son, I love you. Nothing you say will make any difference as to how I feel about you. And keep in mind that I spent two horrific years in Viet Nam, so I probably have a good idea what happened to you in Iraq."

Liam searched his dad's features. He'd forgotten his dad had served. The topic had always proven uncomfortable and therefore had been ignored. Searching, probing, his eyes digging, he stared into greenish-brown pools, replicas of his own, and they revealed adoration. Plain and simple, the man loved him. How could he have failed to remember? How could he have just put it out of his mind?

"I killed, Dad. Young guys, maybe family men, certainly someone's sons who probably didn't deserve to die any more than I did."

"Then why did you kill them?"

He leapt up, leaned over the old man, anger blazing. "What do you mean, why?" Rage was evident in his threatening body language. But his dad didn't even flinch. He looked at him steadily, kept eye contact.

Liam felt himself snap, like a cable expected to stretch too far. He whipped around, shoving his clenched hands in his pockets.

"Shit! How could you ask me that?"

"Answer me, Liam. Why?"

Galvanized by fury, he screamed the words that had blocked his throat and his heart. "Because, for Christ sake, because I had no choice. It was kill them or let them kill my men."

The words burst out fuelled by rage and colored by pain. His lips wobbled uncontrollably and tears filled his eyes. He shook so hard he dropped onto the sofa and lowered his head into his hands. A sob escaped, forcing him to bite down hard on bloodied lips, but the next sob escaped, and so did the next.

Strange warmth engulfed him, easing the agony that loosened his control. He sensed Paul's fatherly presence as if vibes of spiritual medication were being launched from the older man's heart, soothing and so appreciated.

"I heard they wanted to award you the Silver Star."

Disgust rang in his voice. "Yeah... for killing

Iraqi soldiers."

"No, for saving Sergeant Harry Ryan."

"How did you know?"

"I ran into an old friend still in uniform. He congratulated me on my brave son."

Liam shook his head sadly and a sound of disgust escaped. "An award for killing."

"No, an award for bravery and for saving a fellow soldier. Because of you, Harry Ryan is with his family today and not underground in one of those sad graves in Arlington."

The words slowly filtered through his tortured brain. In the depths of his despair, relief began to surge throughout his stressed, coiled body. The stiffness in his back let go, and for the first time in months, he felt able to slouch and totally relax his muscles. Exhausted, he laid his head back against the couch and let the shudders wrack his body and soul. His eyes remained closed while the tears poured steadily.

Finally he sighed, and then he swore. Clearing his throat and letting his hands fall loosely next to him, he lay back exhausted. Peace invaded the emptiness left by the tears. Words he'd yelled out rang in his ears like a litany of defense. *Because he'd had no choice!* A melody of forgiveness stretched from his head to his heart. *Because he'd had no choice!*

He felt the cushion next to him depress, and a hand lifted and cradled his. He grasped the fingers tightly, appreciating the rubs and pats from the other man. Words couldn't have soothed him as much as the touch from his father.

Slowly his head slid down to nestle against the shoulder of the man he'd never understood, or in truth, admired very much.

"Tell me why you let me go?"

"If you're asking why I let you go to war, the answer is because of my respect for your choices. If you're asking why I let your mother rule this house and drive you away from me, it's because you loved your mother and I loved you." The simple words were spoken in a voice ripened by regret.

"Aw, Dad. Why did I blame you?"

"Son, I'm not blind, nor am I stupid. But your mother was my adored wife, and I couldn't hurt her any more than I could hurt you. In my mind, no one had the right to denigrate her, myself included. Even though I knew she did so to me."

"Couldn't you see what she was doing? How she turned me against you, belittling and blaming you for everything that ever happened to her? Why didn't you put a stop to it?"

"How? You tell me how to force someone's respect and love. Beat her? Hurt her feelings? Put her down to build myself up?"

"That's what she did constantly."

A sigh escaped, and the older man lifted their hands to lay a soft kiss on Liam's. "I know. I'll try to explain, but the medical terms are beyond me at the moment. The simple explanation—what you never knew because we waited too long to tell you—was that your mother had a brain tumor that often put increased intracranial pressure on her brain and made her suffer those personality anomalies.

"When I first met her, she was like a beautiful butterfly, flitting from flower to flower, never resting or stopping her search, a constant source of joy to a man who'd grown up in a home full of dour people with sour faces. In the earlier years, I called her my sexy little dynamo. Son, she was something to see. Back then, she treated me like a king." The sigh following lasted a long time. "But the tumor began to grow, and she changed."

Liam saw the tears his dad couldn't hide, heard them in the broken, hoarse-sounding voice, and it became his turn to empathize.

"I wish I'd known her then."

"Oh, you did, son. Didn't you ever figure out why she held your heart and only anger came my way? Because from the time you were born until you were a teen, she put all her energy and devotion into helping you become the man you are today. My only regret is that we didn't sit you down and explain the circumstances."

"I wish you would have."

"I see now that we did things wrong. God's honest truth? Don't know if I would've done them any differently, though. What can I say? I loved her."

The vibrating of Liam's cell phone dancing across the counter grabbed both men's attention. Exhaustion fading, he rushed over and lifted it to his ear and listened.

Then he said, "I'm only a short ways away. Wait for me. I'm coming with you." Liam hit End, unplugged the gadget, and pushed it into his jeans pocket.

"You were right. The artist remembered the place and gave directions. Seems the property was owned by their mother's side of the family and they inherited on her death. It's still listed under the name of Baker and so never showed up on the radar. Good call, Dad."

"Guess they're moving in tonight?"

"Yep. And I'm tagging along for the ride." Liam stopped, and with his right hand, he massaged his neck. Both feet shuffled in place, and the memory of being a little kid surfaced. Finally he spoke. "Thanks, Dad. Can't tell you how much better I feel."

His father stood up, and they hugged like men do who understand each other perfectly. Then Paul slapped his back gently one more time and stepped away. "Anytime, son... oh, and keep me posted. You know I'm interested."

Chapter 22

Sadie had to get away from the crazies. Their cheeriness was driving her nuts. And the continual banter gave her a headache. Begging to be excused, she decided that a walk would give her the solitude she hungered for, the quiet time alone to dwell on the man who never left her thoughts.

To haul Susie along seemed ludicrous, since the dog hated her walks, but this time, for some strange reason, she wouldn't be left behind. Sensitive to the emotions of her favorite people, she must have decided Sadie needed company.

Leashes weren't necessary along the lakefront, but in case there was traffic along the road, Sadie decided to take one anyway. Then she slipped on the matching cardigan to her lovely sundress and grabbed her flip-flops.

It was an evening for romance. Streaks of

rainbow brilliance tinted the blue sky to a vista of wonder that made her catch her breath. The low-flying birds sang their thanks for the beautiful day, and tranquility seeped into her very bones. When thoughts of Liam floated into her quietness, she wished desperately that he were there with her, sauntering, hand in hand.

A vision of their disrupted lovemaking invaded as it had been doing since the night before, haunting her, and she replayed every moment over and over, each time more incensed that the phone had rung. She'd loved being held in his strong arms against his hard chest, and had especially liked the sensation of feeling so petite... and, well, feminine.

Tingles swept over her tense back, spread to tease her breasts, and then gathered with a force to attack down below, where her body still screamed from being abandoned. Doubtless they'd finish off what they'd started, and her mind played scenarios of just how it could happen... when, and where...

She was so engrossed she didn't hear her name being called the first time. The rather pale, overweight fellow had to run right up to her, panting and red-faced, before she realized that another person occupied the beach as well as herself.

"Sadie, it is you, isn't it? I wasn't sure at first, but then I recognized your hair, and I remembered your cottage was close."

Oh, god in heaven, how could you be so mean?

Derrick Slater, the guy she disliked more than broccoli—and she hated broccoli—had appeared like a bad omen, considering where her mind had been. Could she pretend she didn't recognize him? Nah, he'd see through the ploy and have even less respect for her than he'd had before.

"Hi, Derrick." Damned if she'd chatter and be friendly.

"You look... ahhh, great!" He did that disgusting trick with his beady eyes as they scanned her body. "What have you been up to? Married? Kids?"

"Nope..." Who knew disgust could react in such a physical way, like wanting to throw up, for instance.

"Gee, if I'd known, I'd have called."

"Then I'm glad you didn't know." Seriously, pervie? You can't see the loathing I'm not even trying to hide?

"You're kidding, right? You always did like to joke around. We could have a good time together again. Give me your number, and I'll give you a call."

"Derrick, if you were the last sucker left breathing in a world of the dead, I'd shoot myself first." Now she smiled.

A deadpan expression replaced his false jovialness, and she knew it had sunk in—she wasn't joking.

"Once a bitch, always a bitch!" He spat the words, then tried to leave too quickly. His foot caught on a branch; he tripped, and windmilled his arms to stay upright. It didn't work. He landed hard.

Sadie turned away but threw her response over her shoulder. "Once a little prick, always a little prick!"

The shakes struck within a few more steps. Thank goodness the trees would block her from his view. Devastated, she needed to hide. Quickly, she stumbled to her once favorite rock and hugged her knees, which gave her the perfect nest to bury her tear-stained face.

The sicko still didn't get it. He'd made her a laughingstock. Everyone read Facebook, and to have details of losing her virginity plastered all over his page had revolted her for a long time. The adjectives he'd used came back to haunt her—"little butterball," "chubby love princess."

She could almost forgive him if he'd needed to prove his own masculinity, but that hadn't been the case. Back in the day, he'd been buff and his popularity had gotten him lots of girls.

It must have been her fault. She'd been the negative. Not good enough for him or any boy. Fat, pimply, and so unhappy—she recognized the feeling as it flooded over her once again.

"Sadie? Honey? Are you all right?" Bea, in her favorite green muumuu, stood in front of her, dismay apparent in her expression. Susie approached also, whined her disapproval, and then slumped at Sadie's feet.

Sadie sniffed and surreptitiously wiped the tears on the sleeve of her sweater. "Sure, Ma. I'm fine. Wind blew some sand in my eyes."

"Let me see." Bea lifted Sadie's face to hers and examined her carefully. "Don't see any sand, just a lot of pain. Want to tell me about it?"

Sadie wrenched her face away and turned in the other direction, hoping the hint would work.

Not with Bea, it didn't. "Was that Derrick 'Scumbag' Slater I saw talking with you on the beach?"

Sadie's heartbeats seemed to stop, then restart, but revved up to twice their normal speed. "You know... about Derrick Slater?"

"Oh, yeah! We all did. Ever heard about his famous case of the runs when he had to leave the football field in the middle of a game? That was Maggie playing payback. Then the principal mysteriously searched his locker due to an anonymous caller accusing him of drug dealing?"

"And they caught him with a bag of Viagra?"

"Dora went a bit crazy, but what the heck. At her age, it was all she could think of doing."

Tickled, Sadie said, "Where did she get the Viagra?"

"Some things you don't ask." Bea grinned, and Sadie couldn't help herself. She returned it, moved over to give her mother room to sit, and reached for her hand to hold.

"And what did you do?"

"Who mwa?" As her finger pointed at her chest, Bea's expression became as innocent as a bookie's.

Sadie looked at her mother and began to chuckle.

"Well, I might have accidently backed into his father's Lexus when he had it parked up on the point. Seems he had plans to seduce another poor innocent. Soon put a stop to that nonsense, I did."

"You followed him?" Shocked laughter escaped.

"Happened to see him drive by, and I might have been a bit curious as to where he might be heading." The self-satisfied grin Bea wore made the coldness Sadie had experienced earlier fade completely, to be replaced with a wonderful kind of warmth. Knowing she was loved so much woke something up inside.

"I never knew."

"You wouldn't talk about it. We all tried, but you shut down. Trust me, Sadie. It broke our hearts to see you hurting so badly."

"God, I love you, Ma."

"I love you too, my beautiful little girl. You've always been my favorite."

Sadie laughed. "You say that to all of us."

"Yes, and I mean it. Are you still going to go for a walk? I can hold dinner for an hour, if you'd like to do a bit more daydreaming." First she winked, and then she stood and stretched. "I'll open the chips and dip to keep the girls happy until you return, and then we'll cook supper."

"Thanks, Mom. Think I will stroll up the shoreline for a bit." Sadie looked over toward where the land curved inwards. She remembered a lovely farm nestled in trees there. It had an awesome view, and that would be the perfect distance to take Susie for the rest of their walk.

Chapter 23

Sadie and her lazy bloodhound wandered along to a point where the road intersected with the shoreline. Hesitating at the intersection, Sadie stopped to pet her friend before heading back through the high grass towards the water, where the view made walking worthwhile. The noise of the truck barreling around the corner made her jump back to get out of the way.

Stupid idiot, slow down!

She stared at the back of the truck and saw a tiny body in the window, a Pomeranian with the prettiest red coloring—and a face she recognized. Peppi knew her also, and reacted by barking hysterically.

Sadie hurried after the vehicle and watched as the taillights disappeared in the distance. It was travelling at such a high speed she couldn't possibly keep up and therefore had no idea which of the turnoffs it would have taken in the road ahead.

Since darkness was fast approaching, danger lurked in the tall grass and uneven road. She couldn't keep up this pace. She'd have to slow down. Bent over, clutching the burning in her side, Sadie tried to catch her breath. Could the other dogs be with Peppi? Had she accidentally stumbled on the route to the hideout where the thieves were holding the stolen dogs?

If she could find whichever lane they'd turned into, she could call Liam. Maybe he and Stan would be able to send help to rescue the stolen pets.

But there were a multitude of houses along this stretch. How in the world... Hold it. The sweater she wore was the exact one she had worn the last time she'd walked Peppi. She remembered holding the squirming bundle while Liam tightened the collar he'd escaped from to run free for three blocks. Would it still have enough scent for Susie to follow? Was she good enough to be able to find him from inside a moving truck?

What the heck? It was a chance. She had to try. Glancing around, she found the bloodhound had disappeared. *Oh, no! Don't tell me she gave up and went home.* In her excitement, Sadie had forgotten all about Susie. No, there she came, ambling along at her own speed, slow but steady.

"Susie, you sweetheart. I knew you wouldn't leave me out here all alone." Sadie wrapped her arms around multi flaps of skin, ruffled the pendulous ears, and kissed the air above the slobbering muzzle.

For all that loving, she got back a woof and a glare from bloodshot eyes that clearly showed disdain for her exhausted state. The dog sank onto the grass, slumped into a pile of fur, and sighed.

"No, Susie. You've got work to do. No resting until we find Peppi." Taking off her cardigan, she held it to Susie's nose and gave her the order. "Go find."

From the disinterest in her eyes, if the dog could speak, her words would most likely be, "You've got to be kidding, right?"

Sadie couldn't believe it. Susie had papers for being a purebred tracker. Shouldn't all that pure blood be loaded with little tracker genes? And once a smell got introduced and the order given, the dog's need to deliver would become paramount? Not for Susie.

Trust her mom to choose a dud. "Come on, Susie." This time Sadie put the garment right over her face and mashed it onto her nose. "Poor little Peppi needs us! Now go find her."

Susie sneezed. And lay over on her side. This time her disgusted sigh went on forever.

Just then Sadie remembered the granola bar in her pocket. Susie loved the silly bars.

A chunk of treat, another quick sniff, and Susie got into the game. "That's my girl. Go find Peppi."

Howling, Susie took off—straight down the turnoff that curved around the lake to where the pretty little farmhouse sat in the distance. "Okay, Susie, good girl. This must be where they're holding the dogs." As the two crept closer, Sadie heard the distant pandemonium of barking as it wafted on the night breeze.

She had to get closer. "Lie down, Susie. Stay."

Darned if the mutt didn't obey for once. Folding up like an empty fur coat dropped on the floor, she gave an agreeable woof and closed her eyes.

Sadie tied her leash loosely to the nearest tree, fed her the last of her healthy human treat, and moved forward carefully. Little by little, she got closer to where the yard lights lit an enclosure between the barn and the house.

In the distance, she heard men speaking, but until she actually hid behind the picket fence, she didn't know what was being said.

"Damn, those puppies stink. You better get them outta the van and into the barn. Bradford left orders. Five of them need to be groomed and ready to be delivered to the store Monday morning."

"Hey, why me? I hate the little suckers. It's bad enough putting up with the ones I have here. Stupid Pom got loose and took off. Had to drive for an hour to find him... ended up on the beach playing with some kids. I was pissed, but couldn't give the damn mutt what-for 'cause the little snooty-nosed buggers thought it was *so cute*."

For the last two words, the jerk's voice rose trying to imitate a child, but his raspy tone just sounded crude and cruel. "Probably would have blabbed to Mommy if I'd a smacked it there. Let me tell you, when I get through with that blasted animal, it won't be running anymore." Sadie peered over the fence and saw the same truck that had passed her parked next to the van. Peppi's face could still be seen in the window.

"Yeah, well, tell it to someone who cares. I just spent the whole day—all the way from Oklahoma—locked in the van with 25 of those squalling rats, and I've had it up to my ears with their pissing and shitting everywhere. Van reeks like the outhouse on my old place in Kentucky."

A cell phone rang, and the bigger fellow, the one who'd driven the van, pulled it from his pocket and flipped it open.

"Yeah?" His face first registered anger and then compliance. "Okay, whatever. Fine, they'll be ready." He shut the call off, closed it, and dropped his phone into his shirt pocket, then put his hands under his protruding stomach to balance on his hips.

"Boss is on his way. He's bringing Sanders here to pick up the three dogs we collected on our last haul. Wants to get them out to the place and bred as soon as possible. I suppose he'll want to drive the van back. Damn!"

"Guess you'll have to clean it," Walt said with a sneer.

"Not likely. That's your job. Good thing you found that Pom, 'cause he mentioned him specifically."

"I'll get him and tie him in the barn with the others." Walt stomped forwards and wrenched open the truck door without using any precaution at all. Sadie could have told him it was a stupid thing to do, but it was too late. Peppi streaked past him like a jet-propelled furry red cannonball, straight to where Sadie huddled in the darkness.

"Dad-blasted dog!" Walt ran surprisingly fast for a fellow with bowlegs, tight jeans, and a big stomach. "Ahhh... what do we have here?" Sadie turned to run in the other direction, but too late. He grabbed her hair and yanked cruelly.

"Hey, Hank, come see what I found. I gots me a cute little trespasser—how 'bout that?"

"Shit! Just what we need." Hank stomped nearer.

For a second, Sadie wondered if she'd ever be able to cover up the bald spot in the back of her head. "Let me go. I'm here looking for my dog. She and I got separated, and when I heard voices, I thought you might have seen her."

"And that's why you were hiding behind the fence? 'Cause you wanted to ask us about your dog? Then how come you knew the Pom's name? I heard you say Peppi, no?"

"Yes. I mean, no. I don't know the dog, and I wasn't hiding, I was—"

"Enough. Walt, where'd that little mutt go?"

"Hell if I know. He ran straight to this little lady here and then disappeared." Walt had obviously taken a shine to Sadie's hair, 'cause he didn't seem to want to let go of the mass he still held twisted in his fingers.

"We're in a pickle now. Stop messing with her hair and get her into the barn."

Before that could happen, Walt's ankle became puppy-chow for a very angry, leash-trailing bloodhound. Susie, showing a surprising amount of energy, had latched onto skin and bone and wasn't about to let go. Slobber flying everywhere, bloodshot eyes gleaming hate, her incisors gnawed while Walt screamed. He let go of Sadie's hair and flailed away at a twisting, growling bundle of fury.

"You bastard! Stop hitting my dog!" Walt tried to grab Sadie before she leapt onto Hank's back, but he reacted too slowly. Her hands gouged at beady little eyes, and it took a choke hold to get her to behave. Once Hank had her under control, he kicked Susie with cowboy boots and a lot of oomph. She rolled over and quivered, growling at the same time.

The sneer in his voice said it all. "I'll take her, ya big lug. You get that dog there. Might as well add a hound to our bloody group, eh?" He giggled like a girl at his own pun, grabbed a handful of Sadie's hair and headed toward the barn. *What was it about her hair that drew these suckers?*

Walt, disgusted, kicked Susie again, and she quieted. Then he found the end of her still-attached leash and dragged her pulling and snapping behind the other two.

"Throw that hound in with the others and then tie this little one up good. We'll let the boss figure out what he wants to do with her. Then go and get that blasted runaway." Walt sounded as if his patience had fled.

"Okay, honey chile. You come with little ol' Walt, and I'll take good care of you." Walt wrapped surprisingly strong arms around her waist and started to lift. But Sadie hadn't taken all those aerobic and yoga classes for nothing. She let herself go limp, and when the move pulled him off balance, she kicked up with her foot and caught him in a place that would be guaranteed to make him talk in a higher voice for quite some time.

Before she could gain her balance, Hank was on her and wrestled her to the ground. He seized the front of her sweater, lifted her to her toes and bitch-slapped her. Bells rang in her ears like a Sunday morning call to church. *God, that hurt!*

"Quit sniveling, Walt. Get up and find that other dog. We got no time to lose. I'll tie her up. You get that mutt and then clean out the van."

"Give me five minutes with the bitch first." Pain

rang in Walt's voice, which gave Sadie some solace. If she had to suffer, she was glad she wasn't doing it alone. The gladness disintegrated quickly with Hank's reply.

"Later."

Chapter 24

"You and Sadie going together?" Stan drove with an easy nonchalance that gave his passenger complete confidence.

Liam realized he hadn't spoken in quite some time, and Stan might be thinking he was acting a mite strange. He did have an excuse, just not one he could share.

First he'd filtered through the rioting emotions he'd experienced earlier. His dad had helped him more than anyone else could have. Probably his own fault, since he'd never let anyone else get that close.

His old man had made him see that, when it came right down to it, he'd had no choice. The decisions made were under duress, and he'd reacted as a soldier was trained to act. Somehow that satisfied the guilt monster tearing him apart.

He sensed that from now on he would be able to deal with the shame.

Free of the monkey riding his back, his thoughts of Sadie could be allowed. She'd ensnared him, and he couldn't focus on anything but his need to see her again. He could tell her he'd fallen for her big-time and carry on where they'd left off the night before.

After the conversation with his father, he'd come to a decision. A good decision. One he knew would be right for him. And he wanted to share his news with the sassy girl who'd stolen his heart.

"Ahem." Persistent, Stan tried again to start up a conversation. "You still with me here?"

"Sorry, got a lot on my mind." Liam turned to talk with Stan, and a movement in the back seat caught his attention. *"Where the hell have you been? I could have used your help earlier."*

"You swear too much, poopy-mouth. It isn't nice." Johnnie-boy lounged against the back seat, his long hair splayed over the headrest.

"Who gives a sh..." An "I-told-you" grin stopped Liam from finishing his sentence. "I could have used your help earlier. How come you disappeared?"

"I do have other duties. Untying animals, giving emotional support, I'm needed by more than you."

"Hellooo? Calling Liam." Stan's voice broke into Liam's inner exchange. By the time he'd glanced over to an irked Stan and then snuck a short peek into the back again, his angel had disappeared. *Just like the guy to appear when he's not needed and be gone when I have a million questions.*

An answer popped into his head in that annoying British accent. "I'm not here to answer your questions, mate. Just to save your, ahh, butt."

Stan clicked his fingers in front of Liam, his voice rough but kind. "You okay?"

"Sorry. Where were we? Right, Sadie. Yeah, I hope we're an item. She's a good girl. I'd like to spend a lot more time with her. What about you and Greta?"

"Oh, I guess I'll have to marry that one. She's too perfect to throw back, and I couldn't even if I wanted to."

"Oh, why's that?"

"She's got my number. Always knew I'd get caught one day. Never thought she'd be such a winner."

"I know what you mean. Guess when his time's up, a guy's just gotta go quietly, right?" Liam laughed and was pleased at how happy he sounded.

Stan slowed down. "I think we're getting close. Always did want to see Mara Lake, but never took the time to drive out here."

"Mara Lake? Hell, that's where Sadie and her family are this weekend. I was supposed to join them tomorrow."

"Well, Bud, it looks like it's a date you'll be able to keep."

"If we can free the animals and arrest the scumbags who make money off them. Can you call backup in case there's trouble?"

"Yeah, I've been given authority to bring in the local guys, and the humane society is on standby to come in and take over the kennels, and to ensure the animals are looked after and that proper charges are laid against the perpetrators. In fact, they were more than happy to be involved in the operation. Must be pretty dull around this burg most days."

"And that's a bad thing?"

"Didn't say that. The farm shouldn't be too far. I think it would be best if we park here and hoof it."

"Good thinking. Don't want them getting suspicious if they see a strange car."

Liam felt energy building in the same way he'd always experienced before going out on duty. His spine stiffened, and he cleared his mind of everything except what was needed for the next little while.

Stan pulled off the road into a dark switchback, stepped out of the vehicle, and checked his weapon before replacing it in his back waistband. Meanwhile, Liam collected his dark jacket and made sure his cell phone was switched to vibrate.

"Ready?"

"As I'll ever be."

Night had descended, wasting no time once the sun had set. Moon rays, glinting through the trees, cast shadows over the uneven ground. Darkened foliage became nature's weapon as branches mysteriously appeared out of nowhere. Stan crashed around like a complete greenhorn, but Liam's training kicked in. He took lead.

The flashlight helped some, but not wanting to break an ankle slowed them down more. Once they heard the dogs in the distance, they knew they were on the right trail. And the closer they got, the less they wanted to be seen. With the flashlight turned off, the going got even tougher.

Liam held his hand up and whispered, "Stop grunting and swearing. Who knows if they've posted a guard? They could hear you from a mile away."

"I hate this shit."

"What shit?"

"Killer trees." A city man sounding like a youngster on his first camping trip made Liam smile. For him, this was more like a stroll in the countryside.

"Try crawling on your belly through sand hot enough to scorch your camouflage, and all the while ducking bullets."

"Yeah! Whatever... Holy shit, what the hell? Is that a dog?"

Peppi yipped a warning before he leapt from a rock, landing against Liam's chest. Instincts kicked in as the soldier caught and wrapped the little fellow in his arms. He held on to the whimpering bundle of scared dog and surveyed the drastic changes. Branches attached to burrs stuck out all over the wretched shivering pup, his normally fluffy Pomeranian coat filthy with weeds and thistles.

"Poor fella. It's okay, Peppi. I've got you now." Baby talk soothed the terrified Pom, and intuition told Liam it was sorely needed.

"Is that the missing Pomeranian?" Stan reached over to help pull the worst of the branches from the dog's mangled coat. At the same time, he awkwardly patted.

"This is Peppi—the runaway. Smartest of the lot—and trust me, Sadie has trained all these animals on tricks you wouldn't believe."

Liam gladly put up with having his face washed as he cleaned the worst of the mess off the little guy. He must be getting soft. The surprising gush of gladness he'd felt upon sight of the tiny fellow wouldn't be admitted or shared. That loss of "macho" would be his secret.

"Either we'll have to take the mutt along or... or take him back to the car? What do you think?" The hesitation before the last part of his sentence emphasized Stan's choice.

Going back wasn't his option either, and so he followed his gut. "We'll take him with us. If I give him the order to be quiet, he'll listen."

"Good. He came from that direction, so let's go."

"No. The barking is coming from the north."

Liam pointed in the opposite way.

"How would you know that?"

"Trust me. It's my job to know." Liam purposely shook his head and made a sad face. "You city boys!"

"Screw you, soldier."

"Look, I hate to beat a dead horse, but I'm trained to know night noise and how the wind carries—"

"Lead on, then, and quit jabbering." Laughter spread over Stan's face, and the friendly slap on Liam's back settled the issue. Unforeseen delight speared through his innards. It felt unexpectedly good to be part of an alliance once more, and on a mission. It had been such a long time since he'd recognized and embraced such things, he reveled in the re-awakening.

As they approached the property, they saw exactly what Sadie had seen—a yard well lit between the back of a large house and small outbuildings scattered around a bigger imposing structure Liam took to be the barn.

Still carrying Peppi, who'd begun to growl, Liam leaned over to speak softly in his ear. "Peppi, quiet!"

Wriggling, straining, the agile pup loosened his grip, and before he could stop him, the dog landed on the ground and took off running. Knowing they needed to keep him in sight, the two men followed, staying low to the ground and crouching behind the plentiful bushes as they went.

Leaping up on a mound of hay piled next to a barn's small window, Peppi looked in. Agitated, he danced madly in circles, performing for the men. Obviously he wanted them to see what he could see, and both Liam and Stan carefully advanced and looked into the same window.

"Son of a bit—" Stan's hands shut off the rest of Liam's expletive as he hauled him away from where they could be seen.

"Shut up! Stop struggling. If they get us, there'll be no one to help her."

"Screw you. Those bastards have Sadie tied up like some kind of fatted calf. I'll kill them."

"Not on my watch. Look, Liam. This isn't just stealing a few dogs any longer. We're talking kidnapping. We have to call for back-up."

"You do that. I'm not waiting. That's my girl in there."

"You'll do as I say." Steel rang in the voice, authority taking over. "I'll arrest you if you make any move without my say-so. Got it?" Pretty hard not to, when the guy's angry mug loomed two inches away.

Liam took a breath and forced himself to cool down. "Got it!" Many times, he'd been the man in charge. He knew the difficulties that position held without having his men mutiny against his orders. On the contrary, they'd always respected him, and it was that which had saved their asses a number of times in battle.

"You okay now?" Stan searched his eyes and accepted his nod of affirmation. "I'm calling it in."

"What if there are only one or two guys here? We could take them, couldn't we?"

"How the hell are we gonna find that out?"

"I've got an idea. Do you have a pen?" Stan rummaged in his top pocket. "What are you doing?"

"Right now there's only one guy in the back area washing a very unhappy Nicki. He's lucky he has a muzzle on that Shepherd and Nicki's neck held in a holder or the jerk would be mincemeat. Nicki hates men. Another plus, Sadie's facing away from him. He's tied her to the chair but her hands are in front. If I can get Peppi to take her this note, she'll let us know how many there are."

"How the hell can she do that? Her mouth is gagged."

"Watch and learn my friend." Liam gave Peppi the note and an order. "Give this to Sadie. Good boy. Go."

Both men crowded at the dirty window and watched as the dog slunk into the barn and hurried over to the girl. They knew when she caught sight of him by the stiffening of her body. And when he passed over the paper, she caught on quickly. Not being able to see them didn't deter her from following instructions. The dog stayed next to her on the ground and watched for his orders. Soon, they saw him sit, and then he barked twice.

"There are two men."

"You're positive?"

"Yeah!" The surety in Liam's voice made his pronouncement indisputable.

Peppi's barking had alerted Hank, and the chase was on. Finally he cornered the poor little guy and seized him cruelly. "Come 'ere, you rotten pest. Look at the mess you're in. It'll take me an hour to clean you up." He smacked the dog across the muzzle to stop Peppi's furious noises and carried him toward the grooming section in the barn.

Stan held Liam back once again until he calmed down. Then, speaking from the side of his mouth, his gaze riveted on the happenings inside the barn, he asked, "What did you write?"

'I asked her how many men were here," Liam muttered. His eyes stayed glued to the girl who'd stirred up longings he'd never dreamed he would feel.

"How did she tell...? Never mind. You can fill me in later." Stan put his unused cell phone back into his pocket, then backed away from the window and said, "You stay here and watch. I'm going to find the other dude. If I can contain him, we'll go in and get your girl."

Liam nodded. Anger made speaking impossible without howling his rage. He'd never before been so personally involved in an operation of this kind. Fear and hatred ripped away the thin mantle of morality. He felt unbridled revulsion for another human being. Punching that ugly face would give him so much satisfaction that he promised himself the treat before the night was over. And if the asshole touched his Sadie one more time, he'd kill him.

Chapter 25

Gagged and tied to a chair, with no hope of anyone knowing her whereabouts, fear began to settle in the pit of Sadie's stomach. All she could think about was Walt's threat and the hunger in Hank's eyes as he'd tied her arms and then let his hands seek out places to grope and pinch that he had no right touching.

Because he'd taken her sweater off and used it to tie her feet, the rough rope around her bare arms and wrists scraped tender skin—abrading and chafing. Bloody areas were visible where she'd worked at loosening them, and multiple bruises were already forming from the mean handling she'd received.

It didn't lessen her determination to get loose. If anything, that became stronger. Neither one of those two bottom-feeders had given any care for the harsh treatment they'd inflicted. And that alone didn't bode well for entreaties or possible future begging. In fact, she knew in her heart they'd enjoy her all the more in subjugation. Not that she'd give them the satisfaction if she could help it—IF she could help it?

She'd heard of women in these circumstances and had always pitied them, never once imagining she'd know personally the terror they'd felt. To make things worse, her full bladder screamed for release. And the pounding in the back of her head wouldn't let up. Images flashed, and she swallowed the screams forming in her mind. Oh, God!

Her gaze roamed, seeking for inspiration, hoping something hanging or leaning against the immaculate walls could eventually be used for a weapon... anything long and preferably sharp. Those scumbags needed to be taught a lesson, and she'd love to be their teacher.

Little chance of that happening, not with her tied to a chair and a gag stuck in her mouth. Then, like a dream come true, she spotted a hook very near to her chair. If only she could move closer and lift her hands enough... With her attention fully on this endeavor, she didn't see Peppi slink in through the open door.

Once his two front paws planted themselves in her lap, she worried that Hank would see him. It wouldn't go well if the poor little guy got caught. But when he thrust a piece of paper into her hands, she almost fainted. Luckily, when Hank tied her, she'd managed to wriggle enough that he hadn't quite cut off her circulation. She had room to maneuver and read the note.

The relief coursing through her when she read the message—*Sunshine, Stan and I are outside. How many men are there? Get Peppi to tell us. L*—wouldn't be something she'd soon forget. And if she survived this night, Mr. L would be sweetly rewarded, and then some.

Peppi hid by her feet, and she'd swear encouragement covered his little-doggie features. If he barked, Hank might get him. But she knew Stan and Liam needed the information. Overcoming her hesitation, she held up two fingers. After he barked twice, she waved him off—not quick enough.

The rough, fat bastard caught him, and her friend's squeal of pain added more wounds to her already sore heart. What a sorry excuse for a human being! Promises of retribution settled in her head.

Chapter 26

Stan stumbled around the perimeter. With the darkness fully settled, tree roots and branches, rocks, and uneven ground made the going difficult. Thank goodness the glow from the yard lights helped somewhat as he got closer.

Whimpers and cries from agitated puppies could be heard from inside a parked van, and his conscience gave him hell for ignoring those heart-wrenching noises.

He wanted to let them out. But he couldn't... could he? Hey, all those freed puppies running around would bring the other dude into the open. Now where did that thought come from? Temptation overcoming training, he decided to follow his instincts.

He slithered along the side of the van and prayed the front would be unlocked. With this type of vehicle, a lever on the driver's floor would release the back and let him open the doors.

When he checked the lock in the window, the strangest thing happened. At first he could have sworn the lever was down, but right before his eyes, it sprang up. He twisted the handle and, sure enough, it was unlocked. Weird!

Creeping to the back of the vehicle, he quietly peeked inside, and a blast of fetid air hit him dead on. Whew, what a rancid smell! Poor puppies must have been locked in there for hours.

They were mighty glad to see him. Whines of delight from wiggling, ecstatic furballs made him smile, until they threw themselves against the doors. Before he knew what hit him, puppies were everywhere. Yipping and yapping with delight, they ran in circles around his feet and made such a racket that two men came running towards him from different directions, both waving guns and both pissed.

"Who the hell are you?" The dog-washer who'd come from the barn spoke with authority. Stan took him to be the boss.

Deciding to play dumb, Stan flung his arms in the air and tried to look like a normal guy in the wrong place at the wrong time. "Hey, guys, cool it! I'm staying in a cabin down there and was just walking the beach when I heard puppies crying. Thought they were hurt, so I came to see. I'm a sucker for dogs." He used his most appealing smile and prayed it would work.

Obviously he didn't appeal to either of the two in front of him. "Put your hands up and keep them there." Hank motioned to Walt. "See if he's carrying."

Walt came up behind Stan, found the Glock tucked into his belt, and removed it. "Lookie what I found." He waved it around like an idiot, which gave Stan the opening he needed. With a perfect maneuver from his training days, he swung around and whipped the gun from Walt's hand. But before he could swing Walt in front of him, everything went black.

"You idiot! What the hell were you thinking, waving the stupid gun around? You're lucky I'm quick on my feet, or he'da had us. Now stop being so careless... ow!" Hank danced around and lifted his leg with an angry golden retriever puppy hanging on the end of his jeans. "Damn ankle biters! Throw the cop into the back of the van and use the duct tape so he can't get loose. Then help me catch these little suckers before I get fed up and use 'em for target practice."

From the side of the barn, Liam watched the frenzied action happening near the van. Stan was down. He'd come around too late to help him, but he would take this time while the other two were occupied, and get his girl.

Carefully, using the shadows, he slunk along the wall, entered, and moved to where he last saw

Sadie.

Except she wasn't there! Only an empty, overturned chair near a bloody hook and scattered pieces of rope gave any indication she'd been there at all.

Son of a bitch! Where the hell did that woman get to now?

Chapter 27

Sadie, freed by some slick maneuvering and a sharp hook, decided to look for Liam. Observing a back door farther down the barn, she ran, let herself out, and faded into the night. Earlier, she'd noticed the small window, and now she wondered if maybe they'd used that to know where she had been held captive. Cautiously she made her way to where she figured it was located.

No one! A commotion registered out front, and she decided to investigate. An arm around her middle and a hand over her mouth cut off those plans. She fought like a wildcat until Liam's grunts and pleas registered. "Hey, Doll, it's me. Stop that!"

"Are you crazy? You scared the hell outta me." She grabbed his hands and threw them away from her. Then, being her contrary self, she launched herself into his arms.

"Shush! I didn't want you to scream." Once he had her secure, if his groan of relief was any indication, he seemed fairly happy. He kissed her hard, then whispered. "Do you want them to find us? They just caught Stan." As if he couldn't help himself, he kissed her again, his hands cradling her head like he'd never let her go.

"Stan's with you? I guess that was the ruckus I heard in the yard. It sounded like a puppy party in progress."

Liam smiled, his gorgeous dimples appearing just long enough for her to swear that either her heart had swelled or her chest cavity had shrunk. "They have Stan tied in the back of that van. Do you think you could get to him and let him loose? I have some scores that need settling."

"If it's all the same to you, I'd rather settle a few scores myself." She stepped away from his arms and scuttled around, searching until she found a heavy log about the size of a bat and balanced it in her hand.

"Put that down."

"I will not." She brandished it towards him to emphasize her refusal.

"Fine, probably wouldn't hurt for you to have a weapon, but you'll do as I say. Sneak around the back and go to the van. I don't want them touching you again."

"I'm staying with you." She stuck her face closer to his, and in the moonlight, she watched his expression harden. His stance changed—legs separated and his hands formed fists that rested on his hips. His voice, harsh with a steeliness she'd never heard, grated on her already jumpy nerves.

"Have it your way, but this is fair warning. If I see one of them lay a finger on you, I'll have to kill him."

Sadie believed his threat. "Oh, you're such a spoilsport." She stood down. His words produced so much happiness it felt like a sparkler had been lit inside her.

"Come on, I'll show you which way to go." He kissed her again, this time with a lingering sweetness that made her forget her own name. Then he took her hand and led her to the right side of the barn where he'd hidden earlier to watch the shenanigans in the yard.

Nothing had changed much, except now there were two lunatics scurrying around the open space, chasing puppies and cussing a blue streak. As much as Sadie detested the men, she had to admit they presented a comical picture.

From the looks of it, there were Lab puppies, Terriers, German shepherds, Shih-tzus, and fluffy white Samoyeds, a mix of maybe twenty or more, all kiyiying and out of control. Suddenly, headlights appeared as a Lincoln SUV pulled into the yard.

Bradford leapt from the driver's seat, leaving his passenger, Saunders, behind with a comical grin plastered over his face. He halted at the fringe of the hysteria. "What in tarnation is going on around here?" He had to shout to be heard. Finally he got Hank and Walt's attention. "Why are all those puppies running free?"

Hank, with a pup squeezed under each arm, stopped in front of the boss. "Your idiot nephew opened the van and let them loose is what happened. I've been running myself ragged trying to clean up his mess, but these little suckers won't stay still long enough to get caught."

"I can't leave you guys alone for five minutes." One of the pups reached up and nipped Hank's cheek, and in retribution, he squeezed hard enough to make the little Lab squeal in pain.

"Be careful, you imbecile! They're worth a fortune."

Just then, one of the terriers spied Bradford's expensive suit pants and attacked. Growling happily, he tugged at the hem every which way. Bradford lifted his foot and kicked out, trying unsuccessfully to dislodge it.

"Let go, you little sucker, before I get mad." The more he tried to get loose, the more the little warrior clung. "Get him off me!"

Walt skidded down on his knees and grabbed the wriggly mass, but the pup had no intention of giving up such fun. The noise of material ripping barely registered over the rest of the commotion.

***

Sadie's giggles became uncontrollable, and she clutched at her stomach to stop the pain. Laughing quietly didn't come easy, not when happiness pulsed just under the levity, making the emotion so much stronger.

The male laughter close behind her also added to her high spirits. Soon they'd have to make their move, but how could one not stop to enjoy a never-to-be-seen-again moment? "We should go now, before they grab some brains." He had begun to steer her towards the van when another set of headlights raced into the yard and pulled up right behind the Lincoln.

Bea and her daughters lost no time in approaching the others, and from where she stood transfixed, Sadie could see the anxiety on her mother's face change to astonishment. "Is this a private party, or can anyone join?" Bea, never at a loss for words, approached Bradford.

"I'm sorry, ma'am. We've had a bit of a problem here at our kennels. As you can see, some of our puppies have gotten loose. We're rounding them up now and will have peace restored soon."

Sadie saw the scene through Bea and her sisters' eyes. Worry bit in and took a large chunk out of her humor. Instinctively, she made a move to approach, and Liam pulled her back, whispering, "Don't start anything. Have you forgotten about their guns? We need to get Stan and get out of here. The police will return and do their job."

Sadie crouched back down and watched the scene unfold. She knew something Liam didn't.

Never one for mistreating animals, Bea had fought tooth and nail to get proper funding diverted to their local SPCA. Her own animals were babied beyond belief, and any sign of animal cruelty brought out a latent mean streak in her otherwise jolly personality.

Bea hollered to be heard over the din, disgust plain in her tone. "These babies are filthy. They're scared, and you're mistreating them."

"Not at all!" Bradford's loud shock was an Emmy-winning performance. "They've just arrived. We were trying to get them into their new homes in the barn—feed them and bath them. I'll have you know, we take good care of our animals." He puffed up like a broody hen.

Slightly mollified, Bea's stance changed from aggressive to somewhat passive.

"I'm happy to hear that."

"Now, what can I do for you?" The slimy merchant was back in the saddle.

"I'm looking for my daughter, Sadie. She took our bloodhound for a walk a few hours ago and hasn't returned. They were coming in this direction, and I wondered if you might have seen her?"

"Walt, have you seen a young girl and her dog?" Still trying to control the mischievous pant-chewer, Walt shook his head. "Nope! Too busy doing my job and minding my own business."

"What about you, Hank?"

"Nah, I ain't seen anyone like that around here. She's probably—"

Bradford cut him off midstream. He kept his hands in his pants pockets as he rocked on his heels. "Sorry. Can't help you. And as you can see, we have a lot of work to do..."

All the while Bea had been holding the conversation with Bradford, the two girls who'd followed their mom into the yard had knelt down and magic quickly ensued. Seeking a kind voice, gentle touches, and a warm refuge, the pups soon surrounded them. The noise level had lowered to where a person could hear themselves think. Having to scream wasn't a necessity any longer.

Other dogs barking in the distance now registered, one much louder than all the others. A hound's baying has a certain ring to it, and Susie's howl was definitely particular.

Sadie clutched at Liam's arm. "Oh, no! It's Susie. She must have heard Mom's car drive in."

He restrained her. "Don't panic! Let's see what happens."

She broke his hold, got ready to react, but held her position. Her pulse rate spiked. Blood pumped so violently that if a person looked at her neck the throbbing would have been visible.

A soft touch and a soothing "shuu" helped, but just a little. She'd seen the moment when the howling sound had registered with her mom and sisters.

"That is my hound dog. She's in the barn. What the hell is going on around here? Where is my daughter?" Already a big woman, when angry Bea swelled to major proportions.

"I assure you, that is not—"

Bea poked her finger at the man and then buried it in his chest for emphasis. "Don't you lie to me, mister."

Walt, still carrying his brains in his backside, dropped the terrier he'd just caught and pulled out his gun to aim it directly at Bea. "If the boss says it ain't your dog, then it ain't your dog. Now why don't you and your two heifers get in your car and vamoose."

Sadie groaned, and Liam stiffened. But before they could react, Bea had nonchalantly leaned over, and before anyone suspected her intentions, she smacked Walt across his gun arm. What she hadn't seen was Hank's arm lifting to slug her back.

Sadie broke free from Liam's arms and flew from behind the bushes, her club held high. "Don't you touch my mom!" The scream that burst out of her seemed to add power to her legs. She moved like a whirlwind.

She swacked Hank in time to stop him from connecting with her mom, but she'd forgotten how fast the little man could move. His left arm came up swinging.

Seconds before he could connect, Liam performed a karate move one only ever saw in the movies. Flying through the air, his foot kicking out caught the man in his chest, and the weasel went down for the count. Almost at the same time, the soldier threw a punch in Walt's direction, and he flew ass over teakettle. No sooner had he landed than there were two very angry females kneeling on him with no intention of moving.

Back on his feet, Liam turned to face Bradford's gun.

Chapter 28

"Enough! Stop or I'll shoot you, the girl, and... and her mom. In fact, I'll shoot the whole lot of you." Hysterics were heard in the man's screams and visible in his twitching eyes. The way he waved his gun around like a lunatic might have given one an indication of his erratic frame of mind, vicious fart that he was. "You're all trespassing, and according to the law I can protect my property from thieves."

Because of the din, Bradford didn't notice the van doors swinging back, but Liam did.

A very angry Stan stood between the open doors with a small pistol clutched in his taped-together hands. "You're under arrest. Put that gun down now, or I'll bloody shoot you and enjoy every minute." Duct tape had been ripped from his mouth and still clung to one cheek.

Using Stan's appearance to his advantage, Liam

performed a neat trick in which one minute Bradford held a gun and the next his arm was behind his back and the gun safely in Liam's hands.

Liam grinned at the irate cop and said, "What took you so long? I expected you to show up a while ago."

"Yeah! Well, I was a bit tied up, but I came as soon as I could."

Liam teased, "I saw that idiot take your gun away from you earlier." He pointed at the squirming bundle the girls were using as a bench. "Don't tell me he left it in the van?"

"I wish. He took the big boy, but I always keep a smaller spare on my ankle. Guess who was too lazy to bend down."

He grinned and then motioned toward the Lincoln. "Go get the other shmuck, and we'll get them all contained in the barn." He held out his wrists to Sadie, who was wrapped in her mother's arms, and said, "Sadie, enough with the smooching. Come and cut me loose. And ask the lovely lady who's hugging you to call 911. It's way past time to get these guys put away."

Liam approached the Lincoln with care, making sure to hold the gun where it would be visible to the car's inhabitant. Since the fellow seemed to be crouched on the floor, face hidden in his hands, Liam wasn't too concerned, but his training had taught him to always be prepared.

He opened the door and a jabbering fool looked

up, face pasty white as if he'd seen a ghost. Since Johnny-angel relaxed in the back seat, grinning from ear to ear, Liam caught on pretty fast to what the blathering meant about "doors that wouldn't open" and "disappearing pirates".

"I'm shocked you bothered to show up. I know how much you dislike confrontation." Liam couldn't resist a little dig.

"Wouldn't have missed it for the world, mate. I guess you've got things under control now. Cheerio!" Liam shook his head at John-boy's cavalier attitude and annoying disappearing act. Just his luck to get an angel with attitude.

Sanders' subsequent wail at the angel's lingering moronic chuckle made Liam crack up. He hadn't had so much fun in a long time.

He helped the shivering mess out of the car, and from the odor emitted around the dude's backside, it looked as if someone recently had the shit scared outta them, literally.

Approaching sirens screamed in the distance. The racket increasing to headache level as three police cars swerved into the yard, creating a small dust storm.

Chapter 29

Sadie brushed her hair until the pain in her mistreated scalp made her stop, then lightly perfumed her body with her favorite flowery scent. She'd changed her nightwear twice and finally ended up putting on the first she'd chosen—a short-shorts and cami ensemble in turquoise silk—another of her mom's risqué gifts she'd never worn. Good thing she kept extra clothes at the cabin or she'd have been forced to wear what she'd packed—her favorite hockey t-shirt and the old pair of grey shorts that had seen better days.

The mirror, her old friend, drew her as usual, and a stranger stared back. Tousled blonde curls rioted around her face, and the greeny-blue color of her pajamas made her normally green eyes flash the same tones. She looked nice. You could say beautiful, but she wouldn't go that far.

Angling her head different ways, she decided "this look" wasn't her normal style, but tonight did call for sexy, didn't it? After all, she'd invited a man to her room and fully expected to make mad passionate love with him before the night ended. *Please, Lord!* At least she could look nice. Puffing her hair one more time, she stepped away.

Okay. Do I wait here on the chair and pretend I'm reading? She groaned a silent no. *That's so dorky. Right!* She ran to the bed and arranged herself against the headboard. Then she smothered a whimper and bolted, knowing she'd never let him see her acting like such an idiot.

He'll expect me to be in bed, won't he? So I'll just go to bed and leave a light on so he can see where to go when he comes into the room. Great! She turned on the lamp and got into bed. Then she surveyed the room, and the mirror next to her caught her frantic glance.

No, noooo... In this light, her blonde hair, a golden cloud around her pale face, made her look like a very young girl. Not the image she wanted for tonight. She gathered it, trying to pull it back behind her ears, but all the different lengths wouldn't co-operate.

She wavered. *For heaven's sake, relax. You hair looks fine. Now what?* It dawned on her that with the light turned up so high, he'd see her nervousness, which wouldn't do at all.

She ran to her bathroom, flipped the switch, and

closed the door to within an inch, so just enough light would illuminate her in the bed. Then she turned off the lamp and huddled under the covers.

Soon noise from the door opening and closing could be heard. She stiffened as if a gun had been shoved in her back. A dark figure approached the bed and leaned in to lift the covers. "Hi!" His velvet voice alone caused her body to vibrate and flood.

She shifted to give him room and lifted her head for his arm to surround her. Heart thudding, she needed to break the silence.

"I thought those women would never stop rehashing the night." Sadie sighed and cautiously cuddled up next to him.

"To be expected, I guess. Tonight wasn't the kind of evening most folks are used to. Can't blame them for their excitement. But I did hope all the celebratory wine we toasted with would do the trick and help them wind down."

"You don't know my family." She knew her voice reflected some of her pride, but since it was a new sensation directed at her loved ones, it sounded less than what she truly felt.

"I can't believe how many glasses they guzzled and could still talk and walk without slurring or dropping." He shifted around, his pajama-clad legs entwining with hers while his arms scooped her closer, fitting her to his frame. "You slept in this bed when? In grade school?"

"Quit whining! This is cozy."

"Sure. It's not your arse sticking out the side." His teasing mock-grumble made the joy in her swell, then burst. Giggles erupted, and since she'd never been prone to giggles, an abundance had been stored. Once loose, they wouldn't stop.

His kisses did the trick. She found it pretty hard to laugh with a tongue in her mouth. Soon consciousness meant taking a breath, and she gently shoved on his chest to push him away.

Since he'd maneuvered himself to be partially on top of her, he didn't go very far. With the small amount of light reflecting his hungry passion, confusion struck, and then shyness.

Babbling, she said, "What a night. Could you believe the hullaballoo? I swear Mrs. Brill sobbed like a baby when I phoned to say we'd found Giorgio. Seems the reward had been upped to ten thousand dollars, and she insisted she'd be writing us a check for every penny. I told her we'd be happy to donate it to the SPCA. Now that they have so many puppies, they'll need to find good homes."

Blah, blah—it was like a geyser had attached itself to her mouth. First she looked over his shoulder and then above his head.

Being a good guy and obviously sensing her discomfort, Liam placed his elbow near her face, balanced his head on his fist, and his teasing grin said it all. He'd go along—for now.

"Good idea. I need to get one of those pups for my dad. He put his order in earlier today. Figures, now he has a family to look after again and another little boy to love, he's decided the house needs a pet."

Even though they'd never met, Sadie liked Liam's father instantly. From the little Liam had shared with her, she'd sensed they had issues, and she hoped those would soon be resolved. Now that she felt so differently about her own goofy relatives, she was ready to open her heart to his also. "He sounds like a sweetheart."

"Yeah, I've just begun to realize he's pretty wonderful. You do know the old saying, don't you? Like father, like son."

Compliments flooded into her head, but stayed there. Her tongue felt as if someone had ripped it down the center and tied a lover's knot with the two ends. Frustrated, she knew she was nuts about the guy and needed to tell him. Or, at the very least, show him.

Taking her time, she lifted her arms to encircle his naked back, then rubbed her hands over the muscles. Overcoming her reserve, she opened herself. "Don't laugh! But I just knew you'd come and save me at that place tonight."

"How could you know that? It was pure good luck that we found out the information about the farmhouse in time." His fingers stroked her cheeks and then her lips.

"At first when they tied me in the chair, I was petrified. I couldn't move, and I thought the worst.

But I saw your face, and your voice whispered for me to be strong and not afraid. It was the strangest experience." The shudder she couldn't hold back endorsed her words. "Then a hook suddenly appeared on the wall close to me. I could have sworn it wasn't there when I first checked my surroundings." She felt Liam stiffen, and she groaned. "It gets even crazier. The ropes around my arms mysteriously loosened." He started to back away and she added. "You think I'm crazy?"

"No! I'm just so happy it all worked out the way it did. That you got away. I don't think I could have stood it if they'd hurt you."

Sadie heard the truth in his voice. The harsh tone said it all. She looked into eyes that gleamed and noticed the extra shine of emotions he couldn't hide.

That did it. Reaching up, she kissed him like she'd never kissed anyone before. With her heart and soul urging her on, she worked magic.

Chapter 30

Liam had never been kissed in quite this way. Never trembled like a shock victim before, either. Sadie's lips connected to sanctuaries in his body that were secret, safe places. But they opened to her—her spirit and her love—with a welcoming reciprocal emotion, then closed back down with her safe inside.

Forever, she'd be his. And he accepted it without any doubts. This woman belonged with him, and from now on he'd cherish her with every breath he took.

Soon he stopped thinking about anything but giving her pleasure. His tongue searched for hers, and he twisted first one way and then the other in order to taste her better. He swore he could hear her heart beating and, lowering his mouth, he sucked and nibbled on the pulse working overtime in her neck.

No other woman's sighs and moans had ever turned him on like Sadie's did. Losing control, he ground his lower body into hers and then growled with satisfaction when she wrapped her legs around his hips and played tit for tat.

The constricting blankets had to go. He whipped them off at the same time as he moved her on top of him so he'd be free to help her undress. He reached for the bottom of her silky top, but before he lifted it, he searched her gaze. A smile flashed to express his commitment to the step they were taking.

Her answering smile, identical to his, melted everything hard inside of him. Except for one area that just grew bigger, if that was even possible. His need for another scorching kiss took precedence before they moved on but soon her clothes again got in the way of searching hands.

Panting and moaning, she helped him by wiggling this way and that, movements his lower body appreciated. Once uncovered, her full, beautifully formed breasts sat high and firm, the pink tips hard and mesmerizing. They drew him, and she seemed to sense his need. Leaning over him, she let him have full access and then cradled his head while he made love to her chest.

The hungry woman cooed in his ear, and that encouraged more fondling. Soon intense desires demanded he get on with it. Gently he rolled them both to their sides and slid her shorts from her tiny waist and over her hips. He ditched his bottoms while she made friends with the nubs on his chest.

God, she could use that tongue! His body had never swelled to this extent, and the passionate painful intensity made him grit his teeth. Of their own accord, his fingers found her wetness, and he played with her, enjoying her reactions. Never had a woman undulated in quite this way, and his barely-held control slipped further.

Nerve ends screamed for satisfaction. Enough play time. Dazed, he lifted himself and slid her under so she'd be on the bottom. Immediately she accommodated him by straddling his hips and, once again, opened herself to him completely.

He smelled her woman's scent and lost all control. Her entrance beckoned and he penetrated... but slowly—the tightness spoke for itself. She hadn't been with anyone in a very long time, if ever.

With tender ministrations, the wet passage stretched for his sensitized body. He glided in and out—slowly at first, and then faster. Until with hips pumping, he began to move with a rhythm that she copied.

Shuddering—her moans increasing—he came to realize the wild spasms gripping him meant she'd reached her goal. Now, he could surrender. The last push impaled him inside her deeply, intimately. He was home.

Like aftershocks, tremors from inside Sadie

continued, and the sensitized tip of his penis reacted. Waves of pleasure continued to flow. *I've reached paradise!* It was all he thought as his body floated back to earth.

Strength deserted him. Muscles refused to function. Forced to, he dropped his weight on the slight, sweaty, heavy-breathing girl under him. Right now, a baby could take him in arm wrestling.

Her soft mews of satisfaction gave him the utmost pleasure. And so did her arms that squeezed him hard. He'd just been to heaven with this angel. And if he had anything to do with it, he'd be returning there very soon.

Chapter 31

He didn't have the heart to wake her. Curled up in his arms, she slept the sleep of the innocent, her silky hair spread over his chest. Probably the hair tickling is what woke him up.

Carefully he swept the silky mass back from her face and happened to catch the illuminated numbers on his watch. Oh-oh. Mustn't be caught here in her bed.

Moving slowly, he loosened her grasp and shifted himself to the side, where he could slide out from under her warm, clinging body. He'd give a million dollars to stay in the cocoon with her, but he cared too much about her vulnerable nature. As cool as her family were, he sensed that Sadie's new-found understanding of them still needed time to flourish.

If he had his way, and he fully intended to, they'd

soon have a license that gave him rights to her bed. Then, no matter where they slept, he'd never have to leave her again.

His pajama bottoms were on the floor, and he slipped into them without making a sound. He turned to leave, but couldn't. Her essence drew him and he let it. Standing near her side, he loved her a little more with every beat of his heart.

A ping, one he was beginning to recognize, sounded the arrival of his mystical friend.

"She's quite something—"

"Shush, you'll wake her."

"Aye, lover boy, we're not talking out loud. Remember?" Johnny-angel's teasing grin forced Liam to look away.

"Sorry. It's become so normal to converse with you like this; I forget no one else can hear us."

"I've just popped in to say—so long, it's been nice to know ya."

Shock hit him, big time. *"You can't just leave. What if I need you again?"*

"I would venture to guess that your life is on an upswing" The angel's tone lost its teasing. *"My dear fellow, you will be fine from here on out. Once I leave this room, you'll forget I ever existed. We can't have folks running around claiming to see angels, now, can we?"*

Sadness struck, but sense prevailed. Liam knew what the angel said made sense. Still, he hated the idea of letting go.

"You still have a problem?" The rascal stood with

his legs apart and his arms folded. The sleeves of his blousy white shirt draped over the belted narrow waist. For some reason Liam couldn't figure out, the lace on the cuffs didn't seem at all effeminate.

Taking a minute, Liam thought about what his angel had said, and finally he answered. "*You know you're right. Now that I've found my future wife, I'm good.*" He looked over at Sadie, and if a heart could flip, his just performed multiple somersaults. "*And I don't think I'll be having any more sleepless nights after talking things over with my Dad. He straightened me out. And if the nightmares come back, I'll just go and rehash with him again. I've gotta tell you, it feels pretty damn good to know he understands.*"

"*That'll work both ways. You know that, don't you?*"

A few seconds passed while Liam absorbed the full meaning. "*Message received, loud and clear.*" He understood one thing clearly. Who but an angel can make a person commit to not acting like a self-centered jackass?

"*And the future? Your intentions? Will our little Sadie need to suffer a long-distance relationship?*" Censure could barely be heard, but Liam picked it up.

"*No. Leaving her now that we've found each other isn't in the picture. I'm thinking the army has seen enough of this soldier. My plans are to stay in DC and get my law degree—specialize in immigration law.*"

When he smiled, the Johnny Depp lookalike was

the perfect replica of the handsome actor. Seeming to float, he moved over to stand beside Sadie and a visible glow resonated softly around his still figure.

Not wanting to let go, Liam insisted. *"But you're still my guardian angel. You'll come again in case I need you, right?"*

"Probably not, mate. I never was your angel."

Ping!

"I'm Sadie's."

Afterword

Thank you so much for reading *His Devious Angel* – Book #2 of the Angels with Attitudes Series.

I loved writing this story and I hope you enjoyed reading it. If so, I would ask you for a favor. Wherever you purchased this book, please take a few minutes and leave an honest review. Authors enjoy hearing that readers like their stories. Hopefully, others will read your words and choose to buy this book because of your sentiments.

My website at http://mimibarbour.com now has all my books listed with links to the various publishers to make it easy for you to find my other work.

While you're there, I'd really appreciate it if you would sign up for my newsletter so I can keep in touch. I only send out newsletters approximately twice a month including giveaways, contests and freebies, and you have my word that your address will never be shared.

http://bit.ly/mimibarbournewsletter
Hugs, Mimi

My Cheeky
Angel

My Cheeky Angel
Angels with Attitudes Book #1
Can a tomboy change to attract a man?
Naïve and love-starved, Annie will soon to be
celebrating her big 3-0. Something needs to be
done! Celi, her 'down-to-earth' guardian angel

appears to help kick-start Annie's big change—her looks, her job, her whole life. By taking a managerial position with a sophisticated shoe manufacturer, Annie becomes embroiled with her new associates and hooked on the power of big business. Unfortunately, her exhaustion from overwork forces her to ignore old friends. And her lapse places someone she cares about in terrible danger.

Tyler, a Social Worker and a woman-hater previously hurt in two relationships, only wants Annie in his life as a good buddy. Oh yeah! And to help with his mixed-up street kids. Perversely, once her life alters, he misses her like hell. In one sweet night of loving everything changes. But, due to an overabundance of nightcaps, she doesn't remember the night he can't forget.

Praise for My Cheeky Angel:

"I bought this book because I enjoy stories involving friends who end up falling in love. I was not disappointed!" ~ Reviewed by Deborah Hughes

"My Cheeky Angel was my first read, but certainly not last read by Mimi Barbour! This grabbed me from the very beginning and did so until the very end!" ~ Reviewed by sweepingtheusa

Chapter one
- My Cheeky
Angel

Prologue

Chloe the three-year-old tattler tugged at Annie's shirt to get her attention. "Carlton barfed again. His tummy is sick and he's real mad."

"I know, sweetheart, I'll be right there as soon as I get Maggie's ponytail unstuck from the bicycle wheel."

"He's crying for you. He won't let anyone else clean him. Mrs. B. told me you were to come right now. I think she's mad, 'cause her face is all scrunched up."

"You tell Mrs. B. that Maggie is also upset, and I can't leave her. Go on now." Annie's attention returned to the chubby girl whose head was twisted at an awkward angle while strands of her unruly hair were wrapped around the spokes in the wheel.

"Maggie, how in the world did you get your hair caught in here? Hold still, darling, Annie's almost got it. Don't cry now and stop pulling." Annie gave one last yank and the snafu came loose. "There now, you're free. Come here, sweet girl." Annie scooped the sobbing child into her arms. Before Annie could clean her tears, Maggie grunted, heaved and the back of Annie's shirt was covered with the little girl's lunch.

First the stench attacked and then the wet heat soaked through the material. Talk about the proverbial straw. Could this week get any worse?

"Hey Annie," her co-worker, Darlene, called out. "Mrs. B. is about ready to lose it with Carlton. How about a hand?"

"Tell her I've got my own mess to clean up. Maggie's been sick also." Annie imagined herself following up with something like—"Am I the only one here? What is it with everyone lately?"

"It's not our fault you make yourself indispensable to every kid in the place." Then the skinny girl flopped off toward the other room, leaving Annie reeling with the knowledge that she'd actually been voicing her thoughts. Man, she was a mess. A path to her backbone opened and the decision that had been facing her for weeks got made. She needed a change before she came to hate the kids, her day care job and herself. The time had come. Annie Hynes was about to burst out of her cocoon and grow up!

This internal decree lasted until the end of the grueling week and then she began to waver. Old habits kicked in that fueled her insecurities. Should she just up and change, take a new job, be someone different? Lead a life opposite to the way she'd always lived?

Could she?

Chapter One

Today is the first day of the rest of your life.

Annie Hynes shivered as she read the hokey words from the page of the woman's magazine she'd picked up when sleep eluded her. For some strange reason this corny cliché, or one similar, had repeatedly appeared to her in the last several weeks. Actually, ever since she'd decided to change her life and then chickened out.

Each time she'd opened a book, checked the advertising on a bus, or watched a television show, the implication stared her in the face and her suspicion that all these messages were not coincidental really creeped her out.

Her eyes were drawn back to the crinkled page held in her fist. The writing glowed and seemed to be moving in and out. She couldn't turn away. Then the words echoed in her mind like the chorus of a song, sung over and over. She flung the journal away from her, shook her head and gave her eyes a good rubbing.

Okay now, this was really getting spooky. She peered around her room while tiny shivers crisscrossed over her body and woke up her nervous system. Covering her eyes and squirming lower, she snuggled under her colorless beige duvet.

"You can hide all you want but the fact remains, you won't be happy until you change your boring old habits, Annie, my love."

Annie shot into a sitting position and scanned the room again. Not a person in sight. But she'd definitely heard those words. Her tongue glued itself to the roof of her mouth and wouldn't let loose.

"No, you haven't lost them."

"Ha-haven't lost what?" Annie's squeak echoed in the empty room and added to her uneasiness.

"Your marbles!" the raspy voice teased.

Annie scrambled up toward the headboard and hugged herself. "Oh, my god! How did you know that's what I was thinking?"

"Okay, hold onto your big-girl panties. What I'm about to tell you will be hard to believe, but it's true, all the same. I'm your Guardian Angel. Aww, now... Close your mouth, Annie, and don't panic. Look! You can call me Celi."

Annie snorted. "That's it! I'm signing myself in for the works—padded cell, drugs, shock treatments."

The laugh she heard couldn't possibly be described as feminine and musical, more like a rusty smoker grudgingly letting loose.

"You're okay, kid. Because I like you, I'm gonna cut you a break. Look at the end of your bed and don't turn away, no matter what."

Compelled to obey, Annie sat as if in a trance. She watched as a dazzling, misty-like mass seemed to grow in front of her, where the form of a person could be seen slowly emerging. The woman's face and expression came clear before anything else. She looked to be about the same age as Annie. Plain to the point of ugly would be a fitting description—until she grinned. When her eyes lit with unholy glee, anyone near her would have no option but to smile back and fall in love.

Mud-dark hair and deep-set eyes the same color didn't enhance and neither did the prominent nose and sharp-edged cheekbones. In fact, nothing in her face could be called beautiful, or even pleasing, except for the sheer joy in her expression.

"Well? Aren't you the coy one? Most people either faint or have loads of questions." Perched on the end of Annie's bed in a yoga lotus position, Celi waited and watched. Her long shift of luminous white covered all but her bare, pink nail-polished toes.

Annie quickly shifted her feet to tuck them under her, then swallowed repeatedly and wondered if her breathing would ever return to normal. She opened her mouth to the first squeak and snapped it shut before the wail forming could get loose. Since Celi had laughed when she'd knuckled her eyes, Annie didn't go there again. Instead she reached under the duvet and pinched herself.

"Hurts, don't it?" Annie heard the snigger of enjoyment and knew she'd been caught in the act.

"Can I touch you? Are you real?" She reached her hand across the divide, trembled, but kept coming. She had to know if she was seeing things. Or whether a creature called Celi actually sat at the end of her bed.

Satiny-smooth, Celi's skin emanated warmth. And Annie's fingertips tingled once they'd skimmed the surface. "You are real." Her voice reflected her wonder. "I never believed guardian angels existed."

"Think back to yesterday." Celi sinuously waved her hand in front of Annie.

One second she sat, staring at an angel and the next she saw herself, in all her poor-little-ole-me misery, carelessly stepping off a curb on Fifth Avenue. A quick-thinking lady had grabbed her back in time from being pulverized by a speeding blue pickup. Her savior had shaken her and shouted a warning. "Hey, lady, open your eyes. Life's too precious to throw away and too short not to live every minute."

"It was you. You saved me from getting run over. And your words have stayed with me. They've been repeating in my brain, driving me half around the bend."

"Good! I've been trying to wake you up for some time now, but you're stubborn. Your problem is that you refuse to see what's right in front of your face." Celi pointed to the words on the page that miraculously appeared once more clutched in Annie's hands.

She reread the message. "My problem is that I don't want to be me anymore." Whispered out loud, the words held much more power than when they were hidden thoughts.

"Why not? You've a beautiful spirit, Annie."

"But I'm miserable. My life is boring. I'm goofy over a man whose only interest in me is to be his buddy, probably because I look like a guy and—and my job is going nowhere. And worst of all, this month is countdown to my thirtieth birthday."

"So, make the changes you decided on weeks ago. All those motivational speakers you paid big bucks to listen to spouted some wise words. If you don't like who you are—change."

"I want to. I really do. B-but I don't know how." A nagging inner voice wouldn't let up and the singsong refrain of "we're certifiable" wouldn't stop.

Celi chuckled and leaned closer. Her hand lifted and touched Annie's cheek. "No, you aren't certifiable, just scared. Look! You can do it. How many books have you devoured on the subject? How many daydreams have you romanticized?

How many nights have you cried yourself to sleep? What better time than now to make a fresh start?"

"I know you're right." Her thoughts kicked in again and slipped out of her mouth before any idea of shutting up even hit her. "But I can't seem to take that first step. I need help. I'm just plain old Annie Hynes, a tomboy, almost a virgin and—and I've never seen myself any other way."

"And I'm just plain old Celi. But watch what a person can do if they really have the will."

The pantomime being performed in front of Annie left her speechless. First Celi pushed her choppy, straight hair back from her face and magically a brush appeared. She combed it through the ugly color and as it unsnarled the locks, a lovely chestnut brown emerged. Silky waves framed her face like nature had envisioned when the shape had been formed. Next, she passed her fingers over her eyes and her thick, untamed eyebrows recreated themselves to arch perfectly. At the same time a slight hue could be seen to enhance the now sparkling brown orbs. Golden glints sprang to life, accentuated by the added color. Last, she patted her face and faint tinges of pink-toned makeup sculpted her cheeks from sharp to soft, lovely curves. A stunning beauty had replaced the earlier unattractive woman.

"Look closely, Annie. My basic features are the same. I've only brought them to life with cosmetics and tricks. But even those wouldn't be enough for a person to be truly beautiful. You, my dear, were born beautiful. Accept your heart's truth. Make changes, yes! Realize your potential. But what's more important—allow yourself to feel happy. I'll be watching. Talk to me whenever you feel alone or frightened. I might not always answer, but I will listen. I love you, Annie."

Celi blew her a kiss. A serenity of sweetness overwhelmed Annie, leaving her swooning in the loving feeling. Her eyes closed in order to absorb every nuance and when they re-opened, Celi had disappeared.

Annie didn't lie back on the bed; she collapsed. Quivering, while questions raged through her, she replayed the uplifting experience. How many people needed an angel to jump-start them and wake them up to their potential, she wondered? Finally, after reasoning through the unreasonable, she just accepted. The truth stared her in the face—it was past time. If changes were to occur, they needed to be now. Instinctively, Annie knew it. Like a baby who knows the right time to be born, she realized she needed to grasp this moment, step up and be reborn. Or, shut down her inner visionary nagger and her celestial spirit once and for all, most likely with the help of a two-hundred-dollar-an-hour shrink.

Annie let her thoughts continue to roam. And she knew the first area in her life that needed tweaking—her career. She'd always loved being a child-care worker at a prestigious day care center in Manhattan; she felt safe there. Her boss had used the phrase "over-qualified" in an attempt to discourage her from applying in the first place, but she'd begged for the position and had gotten it.

The other girls she worked with were all friendly, but the turnover in staff had made it impossible to get too attached to any one person. Popular girls her age, totally involved with their own full lives, didn't feel the need to put themselves out to the shy girl in their midst. Her friendship mechanism seemed faulty anyway, and her utter lack of self-confidence didn't help in the "making friends" department either.

Her one salvation—the munchkins loved her. With them she could let down her guard, be her jolly self and the more she did, the better they liked it. She'd roll on the floor concocting new games, play puppets, making up characters guaranteed to have them in stitches, and the daily cuddles helped her as much as they settled the little ones. For a few hours each day, life became fun. Tiny loving arms and doting affections were her reward, and, until recently, had been enough.

Guiding naughty fingers away from picking at out-of-bounds areas, singing the same songs over and over and rereading favorite children's stories appeared pathetic as highlights of a workday. Then again, to give up a surety for a vague, frightening future worried the stuffing out of her.

On the other hand, all her schooling was going to waste. The shame of never using the many degrees she'd attained seemed silly. She'd topped the class in every course and left with enough honors to shock her contemporaries.

Recently, she'd been offered a new job, one too good to turn down, but since it happened to be in a totally different field, scaredy-cat Annie couldn't make up her mind. Unsettled, she knew the decision had to be confronted. Tantalized by the notion of meeting new people and making new friends, she fidgeted and hummed, then finally gripped the ragged ends of her short hair and pulled. What the hell was she going to do?

How ironic, she thought. She'd attained her degree in psychology for a specific reason. She'd wanted to comprehend why she suffered from so many fears and why she was happier talking to herself than opening up to others. Clearly it was a crutch. Recognizing the problem appeared to be one thing, but quitting the behavior took on a whole new concept. The hovering loneliness wasn't apparent when she spent so much time in her own head. It remained a wacky addiction, but it worked for her.

Inner silence permeated. Then a familiar rasping voice echoed around her. "Live, Annie. Stop making excuses and stop hiding."

Annie scrunched her pillows behind her neck and lolled against them. The magazine slipped over the side of the bed and flopped onto the floor unnoticed. She wished Celi had stayed longer, but she recognized that the final decisions were up to her. Whether she followed through on the advice had to be her choice.

How can I ever tell anyone what just happened? Nope, probably shouldn't, especially if I don't want to be rushed into a psych ward and spruced up with a garment of the white wrap-around variety. Giggling with slight hysteria, she covered her mouth and scanned the room, just in case.

Her beige, unadorned bedroom loomed in her vision and bugged her. Not enough to make changes, but enough to indicate that her decorating motivation followed everything else in her life—dithering, and procrastination being her preferred course. What a loser!

She tried to imagine the space reflecting a sophisticated, modern look—maybe chocolate browns mixed with turquoise for a little zing, or an all-white room with red splotches, like on the cover of the latest home decorating magazine. Since she could never make up her mind, the beige remained, right down to the colorless decorative vanilla candles.

All of a sudden, the aggravating alarm pealed and woke her from her doze. Instinctively she grabbed her chest to keep her heart from bursting out. Then she flipped to the side of the bed and grappled with the snooze button. "Blasted annoying thing." Flopping back against the pillows, she reminisced over her crazy imagination.

She scoffed. "My own guardian angel! For heaven's sake, what next?" Then her eye caught the torn-out page of her magazine—folded to highlight the words that had started everything. The paper lay on the pillow next to her, propped against the loveliest yellow rose she'd ever seen. The petals, translucent in the streams of sunlight from her uncovered window, urged her to touch and when she did, she heard Celi's husky voice reverberate in the empty room. "Yellow roses symbolize new beginnings, hope, friendship and joy. Now—go get 'em, girl."

Her head fell forward into her hands. Everything from earlier came back to her. The discussion with Celi and her imaginings, even the decisions she'd grappled with. She re-thought her way through the maze again and tried to beat back her misgivings.

The snooze kicked off once more and this time she slapped the alarm off. But the noise had reminded her that Tyler Jones, her best buddy—okay, her only buddy—expected lunch prepared for him today. She'd run out of gas yesterday, fourth time this month, and quesadillas were his payment for her bumming a ride to work.

Tyler. Another looming problem that needed to be solved. Annie knew her reliance on his good nature had to stop. Forcing situations for him to pay attention to her also had to stop. He had no interest in a girlfriend; he'd made that clear right from the beginning. Her tomboy ways and lack of feminine wiles were her major attraction for him, as he'd reiterated numerous times. They were buddies. That she was gaga over him didn't matter. He didn't want romance, not after the last vicious bitch had gotten through with him.

Still into daydreaming, Annie luxuriated in her warm bed and concentrated on Tyler. Aware of the silly lovelorn grin slathered over her face, she shrugged and accepted her addiction. He was the one true-blue person in her life, and she couldn't stop fantasizing about him one day looking into her eyes and falling madly in love.

Over the months, his apartment downstairs had become her problem-solving depot. It beckoned her each time she had troubles. She spent a lot of time there. Tyler, with his straight-shooter answers and his no-nonsense approach to problems, cut through all life's BS. He helped her focus on the positive with such insight as to make her assume the resulting clearness had been hers all along. Probably had something to do with the fact that, as one of the city's best youth social workers, he counseled the mixed-up and downtrodden all day long and relished what he did.

Why she continued to dream of the unattainable, of him and her together, she'd never know. It wasn't as if she could ever see herself being able to participate in any kind of a sexual relationship anyway. Not even with Tyler. That part of her remained shut off, closed down for repairs, ruined.

Tears gathered, but she refused to give in to them. She'd slept on damp pillows too many nights and the futile exercise had accomplished nothing. Like Celi said, the time had come to move on, stifle the worrier and let the stronger side of her personality call the shots, make some changes—live.

The doorbell's pealing interrupted Annie's inner dialogue. The hands on the clock mocked her, proof she'd dawdled yet again. She scrambled from under the covers, retied the ribbon on her droopy, puppy-patterned pajama bottoms and raced to the padlocked entry. Her hands tousled her hair to get rid of the bed-head look and scraped at her eyes before she reached for the knob. First, peeking through the peephole, her customary habit, she pulled the door open a fraction, stretching the chain.

"Ty, I'm really sorry. Could you give me another half an hour? I slept in."

Loveable
Christmas
Angel

Loveable Christmas Angel
Angels with Attitudes – Book #3

Aloha! Sweet romance, lovable angel, and a prickly little boy's Christmas wish.

Christmas in Hawaii! How lucky can a girl get?

Except Leilani is bringing her mother's ashes home to Waikiki and has an urgent plea of help from an aunt she's never even met. After winning two free nights in prestigious Hotel Jordan, things take a turn she never expected. First she gets stuck in an elevator with the prickly, but luscious Mr. Jordan. Secondly, her aunt is a sick woman and only held on for one reason. She wants to pass on her most precious possession – her five-year-old grandchild. The same little fellow that takes one look at Leilani, slaps his fist on his hips and yells, "Go away!"

Kale is the owner of the Jordan Hotel Chain and he can't believe his rotten luck. He broke up with a spoilt brat of a girlfriend and now he's stuck in an elevator with a big-eyed, effusive tourist. How in the world can a guy who's so worldly get hooked on a lively beauty with more dilemmas than anyone he's ever met?

Praise for Loveable Christmas Angel:
***** 343 Reviews – with a rating of 4.6 out of 5 stars
"This book is a must read... it's one of those make-me-feel good type of story that I would highly recommend."- Reviewed by Gisele
"I cried happy tears at times and the ending was a very happy surprise. " -Reviewed by Connie R. Goodall

About the author:

Author, Mimi Barbour

Mimi is an incredibly busy New York Times, USA Today and award-winning, best-selling author who has seven series to her credit.

She lives on the beautiful east coast of Vancouver Island and fills most of her day with writing and promoting her work. The rest of her time is spent in her garden, doing minimal housework and enjoying her husband's company while he cooks their dinner.

"The favorite part of my job is meeting the characters from each new book. Creating them the

way I want and having them act however I think
they should. It's thrilling. Especially when most of
my make-believe folks are interesting, witty and in
most cases, people I would love to know."

Contact Information:

Drop me a line anytime!
I love hearing from my readers.

My website: http://www.mimibarbour.com/

Or my blogspot: http://mimibarbour.blogspot.com

Or follow me on twitter: https://twitter.com/
MimiBarbour

Or on Facebook: Mimi Barbour Fan page

Please sign up for my fun Newsletter: http://bit.ly/
mimibarbournewsletter

www.ingramcontent.com/pod-product-compliance
Lightning Source LLC
Chambersburg PA
CBHW050018180626
46810CB00002B/473